Thanksgiving, 1942

a novel by
Alan Simon

the sequel to
The First Christmas of the War

Thanksgiving, 1942

Second Paperback Publication 2016

First Edition

ISBN: 978-0-9857547-1-6

PERMISSIONS

Cover photograph of the two girls from private family collection.

Cover photograph of soldier compliments and courtesy of the C.E. Daniel Collection / www.danielsww2.com

By Alan Simon

An American Family's Wartime Saga (Series)
The First Christmas of the War (2010 – special Pearl Harbor 75th
    Anniversary Edition with new bonus content, 2016)
Thanksgiving, 1942 (2012)
The First Christmas After the War (2015)
The First Winter of the New War (coming soon)
Additional titles to follow

___

Unfinished Business (2010)

___

Gettysburg, 1913: The Complete Novel of the Great Reunion (2015 – USA Today Bestseller)

Visit Alan Simon's blog about the real-life Gettysburg, 1913 Great Reunion: gettysburg1913.wordpress.com

___

Clemente: Memories of a Once-Young Fan – Four Birthdays, Three World Series, Two Holiday Steelers Games, and One Bar Mitzvah (2012 – Nonfiction Memoir)

Visit www.alansimonbooks.com for new releases and book extras

To be notified by email about future books: info@alansimonbooks.com

"The final months of this year, now almost spent, find our Republic and the Nations joined with it waging a battle on many fronts for the preservation of liberty. In giving thanks for the greatest harvest in the history of our Nation, we who plant and reap can well resolve that in the year to come we will do all in our power to pass that milestone; for by our labors in the fields we can share some part of the sacrifice with our brothers and sons who wear the uniform of the United States."

President Franklin D. Roosevelt,

Proclamation 2571, Thanksgiving Day, 1942

Dedication

When I wrote **The First Christmas of the War** *back in 2002, I began by dedicating that novel to my great-uncles – the real-life sons and sons-in-law of "J. Weisberg & Sons" whom I had given "cameos" in that first novel. The words I had used at that time paid tribute to them for having "sacrificed much of their youth to the Second World War." Several of those great-uncles were still alive at that time, while others had passed on.*

Now, a decade later, all of my great-uncles are gone, as are all of my great-aunts from that branch of my family as well as my grandparents. Therefore, I would like to dedicate **Thanksgiving, 1942** *to the memory of each of them; members of the acclaimed "Greatest Generation," whose perseverance and sacrifices through the hardships of The Great Depression and World War II made it possible for me – as well as hundreds of millions of people around the world – to have lived a life of freedom we otherwise might not have enjoyed.*

Author's Note about Newspaper Headlines and Stories

All of the headlines and newspaper stories from the *Pittsburgh Post-Gazette* and *Pittsburgh Press* used as part of the story line of **Thanksgiving, 1942** are genuine and actually appeared between November 21st and November 27th, 1942.

<u>**For the most part, no artistic license**</u> (for example, shifting of dates; imagined news articles that didn't actually appear; or changes in headline wording) was taken by your author in the interest of story or character development. Rather, each headline referenced contained the exact wording used in the story, and each news story did appear in the specific daily newspaper and on the same date mentioned in the novel.

A Note about the Period Usage of the Terms "Air Corps" and "Army Air Forces" in this Novel

The United States Army Air Corps became the United States Army Air Forces (USAAF) in 1941, and our characters Jonathan and Joseph Coleman are, as indicated, going through training to become USAAF pilots at the time this novel is set. However, the USAAF was frequently referred to by its predecessor's name of the Air Corps by many Americans – civilian and military alike – during the early 1940s, largely for reasons of familiarity because that change had happened so recently. Thus throughout this novel your author frequently switches between the terms "Air Corps" or "Army Air Forces" in dialogue and in the thoughts of various characters, as those alive at the time would likely have done themselves.

(One can find very technical explanations on the Internet that the Air Corps actually still existed administratively even after becoming the Army Air Forces, and wasn't officially disbanded until 1947; but this goes far beyond any realistic explanation why, for example, Jonathan Coleman is mentioned by another character as soon heading off to "Air Corps training.")

Prologue- Saturday Morning, November 21, 1942

Charlene Coleman had a secret. And like most secrets of young women, this one cried out to be conspiratorially shared with a trusted confidante.

"I might be going to Hollywood!" she excitedly blurted out to her cousin Lorraine Walker as seventeen-year-old Charlene and her year-younger cousin sat on Charlene's bed, the door to her bedroom closed to give the girls the privacy they wanted.

"Really?" Lorraine replied in tones just as enthusiastic as those of her cousin's proclamation.

"Yes! You know how I'm in the All-City High School War Bond Benefit in a couple of weeks on the anniversary of Pearl Harbor, right?"

"Uh-huh…"

"Well, we were doing rehearsals yesterday afternoon with all the schools' performers together, and we were over at Peabody?" Charlene continued in her pleasant sing-song voice, referring to Peabody High School, her own Schenley High's cross-town rival in the East End of Pittsburgh.

"Uh-huh?"

"Well, my first number is a duet with Sammy Canter from *Pal Joey*; you know, the musical from last year? That song *I Could Write a Book*?"

"Uh-huh?" Lorraine repeated yet again, enraptured in her cousin's story.

"And then right after that I have a solo from the same musical, that other song: *Bewitched, Bothered, and Bewildered.*"

An anxious nod from Lorraine before her cousin continued.

"Well, guess who was in the audience watching rehearsals!"

A puzzled look on Lorraine's face; no answer forthcoming.

"Come on, guess!" Charlene pleaded, impatient to continue with the story and convey her big news.

"I don't know," Lorraine finally said, shrugging. "Irving Berlin?"

"No-o-o…"

A light bulb went on in Lorraine's head.

"George S. Kaufmann? He's from Pittsburgh, right?"

"No," Charlene answered, her voice rising in excited anticipation. "But you're getting close!"

Lorraine waited a few more seconds, then finally shrugged in frustration.

"I give up, I don't know. Who?"

"You know Gene Kelly? He starred in *Pal Joey* on Broadway?"

"Oh, that's right!" Lorraine's eyes lit up, the image of the dashing Broadway dancer and singer immediately bursting from an imagined fan magazine. "He graduated from Peabody, didn't he?"

Charlene enthusiastically nodded her head.

"That's right! He was in town and stopped by his old high school to watch rehearsals. And there I was with

Sammy Canter, doing the very same number that Gene Kelly and Leila Ernst did every night on Broadway and then right after that, the other one that Vivienne Segal sang!"

Charlene paused for a few seconds and visibly swallowed, as if she needed to prepare herself for what she was about to say next.

"After we were done Sammy and I were backstage, and here he comes walking right up to us: Gene Kelly himself! I didn't know what to say to him but he started talking to us – mostly to me – and Lorraine, I swear I can't remember a thing for about two minutes' worth of what he said to me and what I said back to him. I know we were talking back and forth but like I said, I can't remember anything!"

Lorraine had brought her palms up to her cheeks and her mouth was wide open in astonished admiration of her cousin.

"But then he said to me, and this part I remember word for word; he said: 'Little girl, I can see you have a great deal of talent; I really mean that. You already sing almost as well as Vivienne Segal and Leila Ernst, and you should be out doing War Bond shows all over the country. In fact, you should be out in Hollywood, that's where all the action is these days. I've been out there for a little more than a year now and I tell you, that's where it's all happening. I can see you in the movies…' "

"Oh my God!" Lorraine nearly screamed. "Gene Kelly thinks you should be a movie star!"

"I know!" Charlene gasped. "I could hardly believe it! He gave me his calling card and told me that he was leaving Pittsburgh today for a War Bond tour down south and would be back in Hollywood right after Christmas, and that he wanted me to write him then so he would start asking around to see if one of the studios would bring me out for a screen test. I mean, even now I still think it was all a dream..."

Lorraine's eyes narrowed.

"Maybe he was just...um, you know, maybe he just likes you and wants..."

Charlene shook her head, almost violently as if in denial.

"No! he's married! He married Betsy Blair last year, so it's nothing like that!"

Charlene always knew the latest Hollywood and Broadway news and gossip from reading *Photoplay*, *Modern Screen*, *Picture Play*, and whatever other magazines she could get her hands on.

Lorraine nodded slowly, figuring it was best to let this thread of discussion pass by. She was only sixteen years old but she knew how men sometimes were, married or not: not all that different than the boys from Schenley and other high schools across Pittsburgh and elsewhere, who might have a steady girlfriend but still get their heads turned by just about any other pretty girl.

Then Lorraine had another thought.

"Does your mother know yet?"

Charlene's mood visibly darkened.

"Not yet," she said in much quieter, much more subdued tones, her eyes downcast. "I haven't told her that I met Gene Kelly, I don't even think she knows who he is."

Lorraine hesitated before asking,

"What do you think she'll say?"

Charlene shrugged.

"I don't know…"

But both girls knew exactly how Irene Coleman would react if and when her seventeen-year old daughter approached her with the news that Charlene had just shared so exuberantly with her cousin.

The girls heard footsteps immediately outside Charlene's bedroom door and a second later they saw the knob turn and, as if summoned, in entered Irene. Each girl instantly had the same thought: Charlene's mother had overheard their conversation and there would now be a confrontation similar to the one nearly a year ago when she had learned of Charlene's secret engagement to Larry Moncheck.

"Girls, I need your help in the kitchen in fifteen minutes." The words were spoken in pleasant, even tones but the command was unmistakable.

"Okay," Charlene replied cheerfully; relieved. She knew her mother well enough that if the woman had overheard the talk of Charlene's having talked with a real-life Broadway star about Hollywood, that topic would have been raised seconds earlier.

And that was all. Irene departed as quickly as she had glided into her daughter's room and the cousins were alone again.

* * *

"My God, I have so much to do today!" Irene Coleman thought to herself as she was closing her daughter's bedroom door and turned to head back downstairs.

Dusting and cleaning, the laundry, taking her ration stamps down to the corner market and the butcher shop and the bakery…but top of mind right now was the task for which she had requested – demanded – the assistance of her daughter and her niece: baking pumpkin and apple pies for Sunday dinner.

Her boys were coming home tomorrow! They were scheduled to arrive at Pittsburgh's Penn Station sometime around 8:00 Sunday morning, and for this reason the Coleman family would attend the late Mass at Saint Michael's shortly after Jonathan and Joseph arrived. If their train was delayed, and if the Colemans marched into Saint Michael's a tad late, then so be it. It wasn't every day that her sons were due home from their Army Air Forces training field on furlough over the Thanksgiving holiday!

A feast was called for tomorrow, even with Thanksgiving only four days away. She had carefully parceled out the stamps from the family's ration books to allow for as grandiose of a banquet for Sunday dinner as could be mustered: roast beef, ham, potatoes, turnips, carrots…and much more. No turkey; that would of course wait until Thanksgiving Day. But in almost every other aspect, tomorrow's Sunday dinner would be an earlier version of the holiday feast later this same week. Much of the meats and produce and bread had already been gratefully (and greedily) secured but another round of the markets awaited Irene this afternoon after she and the girls began their baking.

Her thoughts involuntarily wandered to the many months it had been since she had seen her two older sons, and as always the idea greatly saddened her. Irene brusquely forced the notion from her mind. There would be plenty of time for sadness in the days ahead after the boys departed Pittsburgh back to their training base at

Thunderbird Field far away in Arizona, and then of course when they went overseas to fight. For now – for today, for tomorrow, for most of this next week – she would do her best to keep sorrow at bay.

* * *

Gerald Coleman wiped the sweat from his brow. An odd, unseasonable gesture, he thought, considering how low he kept the temperature in his little shoe shop. Heating oil was now strictly rationed by the Office of Price Administration as of a month ago, and if he were to think about it the air temperature inside the shop had to be under sixty degrees on this frigid late November Saturday. The temperature was twenty degrees colder than this time yesterday but still, Gerald was perspiring as if it were an unseasonably warm early autumn day a month or more earlier.

No doubt his perspiration was caused at least in part by the rapid pace of the work in which he had been steadily and energetically engaged since seven o'clock this morning; more than four hours now. He desperately wanted – needed – to finish the handiwork on his son Joseph's brand new baseball glove that would, along with the one he had completed a week ago for his eldest son Jonathan, be the boys' early Christmas gifts. Both boys would be gone long before Christmas arrived this year – the second Christmas of the war – and so for the Coleman family, the same as for thousands of families elsewhere across America who had sons home from military training on furlough, the Thanksgiving holiday of 1942 would also double as a surrogate for Christmas for the boys.

Gerald's thoughts flashed back to last year's Christmas. With the little bit of extra money the family had available for Christmas presents they had bought two new baseball gloves: one for his other boy Thomas, and one for Joseph. When he received Joseph's letter from basic training saying that his mitt had been stolen, Gerald immediately decided that a replacement glove was in order, as well as a brand new one for Jonathan. Unlike last year, these Gerald would make by hand in his shop. No doubt after the boys finished their training out in Phoenix at Thunderbird Field and were sent to airfields in England or somewhere in the Pacific there would be at least a bit of time for pickup games with other Air Corps men. Gerald had seen such pictures in *Life* and *Look* (plus snippets from more than one *Movietone* newsreel) showing pilots, aircrew members, and ground crew men throwing around baseballs and taking turns at bat in between missions.

Gerald knew enough from his own days in the Great War that wartime service was hardly a matter of baseball games and dallying with foreign girls. While those diversions did exist for many soldiers and sailors, the terrifying truth was that before too long both of his sons would likely be regularly placing their lives on the line as they carried out one dangerous mission after another. Both boys were doing their best to become United States Army Air Forces pilots, and so far in this war the USAAF was bearing a significant share of the fighting and dying. Gerald had been fortunate back in '18 to never have seen combat while he had been "Over There" but he sadly knew his sons' wartime service would be different.

Just as his wife Irene was doing at that very same moment back at their home several blocks away, Gerald shook the thoughts of worry and dread for his sons' safety from his head. Instead he thought of his nephew Marty across the world aboard the *USS Augusta*, taking part in the invasion of North Africa since early November. As far as they all knew, Marty was safe; there had been no word of harm coming to the *Augusta* during the offensive. Yet Gerald knew that with much of the war news heavily censored, no parent, brother or sister – or Uncle and Aunt – could be certain of a loved one's safety until he showed up for good at his family's doorstep, duffel bag slung over one shoulder and discharge papers in hand. Whether that day would come for Marty – and for Jonathan and Joseph as well – next year or in 1944 or even further out, nobody knew for certain. And every day that passed until a warrior's return was one more day that those left behind at home needed to worry.

Again, the head shaking and the determination to put these thoughts out of his mind. He forced his attention back to Joseph's baseball glove that was nearly completed, and once again conjured up the image of his beaming sons stepping off the troop train at Pittsburgh's Penn Station tomorrow morning.

* * *

Aboard the *USS Augusta*, Marty Walker relaxed in his bunk, one day's sailing away now from Morocco and North Africa. There was always a chance a sudden return could be ordered but the cease-fire between the Allies and the Vichy French was now nine days old and holding. *Operation Torch* was now well underway and Task Force 34, the western-most element of the Navy's ships supporting the engagement, had been ordered to depart.

Bermuda was their destination, and barring any unforeseen detours or undesirable complications – such as a U-Boat attack – they were scheduled to reach Bermuda on the 26th, Thanksgiving Day, on their way back to Norfolk. A special Thanksgiving celebration was in the works for the *Augusta's* officers and sailors, and while Marty would of course rather be present at the Coleman-Walker Thanksgiving Day gathering no doubt planned at his family's house back in Pittsburgh, this sure would be a damn sight better than celebrating the holiday somewhere in North Africa like the Army men taking part in *Torch* would be doing.

The thought of the soldiers and the invasion itself made Marty think again of that Army General Patton who had come aboard the *Augusta* in late October along with Admiral Hewitt and Admiral Hall. Patton initially directed the invasion from the ship before going ashore himself, and what a character that Patton was. Marty served as a radioman in the Captain's Bridge and had had plenty of opportunity to observe the General and the Admirals up close and personal while on duty. Every so often Patton would allow himself a tight smile or brief laugh but for the most part the man was all business. Marty couldn't help but think if other Generals in the Army were like him, now that they were finally taking the fight to the Nazis there might be hope yet for beating Hitler and Rommel and all of them.

Marty forced himself up in his second-tier bunk, swung his legs over to the side and slid to the floor, careful not to wake the sailor beneath him or the many other sleeping sailors around him. His duty day wouldn't start for three more hours but he couldn't sleep. He decided to head up to the deck to get some badly needed fresh air and watch the *Augusta* steam back towards Bermuda, knowing that the United States would come next. When the ship arrived in Norfolk he would be able to come ashore and he could then make a long-distance call to his parents and his sister Lorraine. He desperately missed his family, and even though he felt a sense of pride and accomplishment for having played a role in such a crucial assault against the Axis in North Africa, he wondered if he had really made the right choice finishing high school early and badgering his father into allowing him to sign up for the Navy.

He forced those thoughts, that second-guessing, from his head. Nothing could be changed, so no sense in giving it another thought. Marty Walker had now been to war and would no doubt do so again and again in the months and years ahead.

* * *

Joseph Coleman was snoozing as the passenger train pulled into St. Louis shortly before noon. His older brother Jonathan was wide awake, though; sleep had been nearly impossible for him since their first train pulled out of Phoenix two evenings earlier. More than two-thirds of the way home now, Jonathan thought to himself. He thought about nudging his brother awake but decided to let him stay asleep if, indeed, Joseph could sleep through the bustle of passengers coming and going up and down the aisles for thirty minutes or so.

For Jonathan, the entire trip home thus far had been consumed by thoughts of Francine Donner. His mind insisted on replaying over and over the tragic scene last Christmas Eve when he had gone to her house to give Francine the engagement ring he had bought two days earlier. Francine's disarming, bubbly chatter when he first arrived, followed by the pained look that had come to her face when she realized what Jonathan's Christmas present for her actually was. Then the blurting out of her shameful secret of having gone all the way with Donnie Yablonski – Jonathan's close friend, and Francine's boyfriend before Jonathan – the previous Saturday night during a reluctantly agreed-to "friendly goodbye date" before Donnie shipped out to basic training shortly after Christmas.

Then, that encounter with her shortly after Saint Valentine's Day…

Much as his mother and father and cousin Marty were each doing at more or less the same instant for their own reasons, Jonathan rapidly shook his head to force away the unpleasant thoughts that had once again insisted on playing out in the theater in his mind. He forced his sights to the train platform and the dozens, maybe even hundreds, of uniformed soldiers and sailors he could now see. He gazed at their faces; not to see if he recognized anybody but rather to build an overall story line in his mind for what was happening to them all.

America had gone to war. *All* of America had gone to war. Last Christmas, the attack on Pearl Harbor had occurred only weeks earlier and the shock had barely worn off as the Coleman family, along with nearly every other family around Pittsburgh and across the country, began adjusting to the new reality of life at war while doing their best to celebrate the holiday season. Now, eleven months later, the entire country had almost fully shifted to a war footing. Uniformed men and boys abounded; not just on an Army Air Forces post like Thunderbird Field, but here on the platform of the St. Louis Union Station…just like the train platforms in Albuquerque and Amarillo and Oklahoma City and dozens of other small towns he had never heard of but which had been other stops along the way. Also, aboard the train itself: nearly three-quarters of the train's passengers at any time were wearing one uniform or another. Most of them were around Jonathan's age, he reckoned, but more than a few were older: late 20s, even 30s and even a few soldiers and sailors that looked to be almost as old as their own father.

And nearly every one of them was new to military life within the past year, courtesy of the "invitation" from Tojo and Hitler. No doubt about it, Jonathan thought again, America had fully gone to war as Thanksgiving Day of 1942, the first Thanksgiving of this new war, approached.

1 – Sunday, November 22, 1942

"Pittsburgh! Pennsylvania Station! Penn Station… Pittsburgh…" The train conductor's voice, trailing off now as he passed down the aisle heading away from the Coleman brothers, slowly brought Joseph out of his surprisingly deep snooze. He had been briefly awake two hours earlier, just before 6:00 A.M. Eastern War Time, but then willed himself back to sleep to fight the dark chill that permeated the train. Now, official sunrise still a quarter of an hour away but light already seeping into the railroad car as the sun's rays peeked above the eastern horizon, the conductor's words told him that falling back asleep was out of the question.

He turned towards his brother Jonathan who was looking out the window and started to speak, but the stale cottony taste and feel in his mouth caused Joseph to swallow a couple of times before croaking out:

"We there?"

Jonathan looked back from the window at his younger brother.

"Almost," he answered. "Just about to cross the Monongahela, should be at the station in about 5 minutes."

Joseph rubbed his eyes with the thumb and forefinger of his left hand. When he had finished he looked over at his brother, who had turned again towards the window on the right side of the train and from the angle of his head appeared to be staring downwards towards the river.

"You sleep at all?" Joseph asked. He knew his brother had been awake every time he had woken during the night, and surmised that Jonathan had gotten little or no sleep.

"A little," was Jonathan's reply; slightly muffled since this time he didn't turn back from the window to look at his brother while talking.

Joseph let out a big yawn, then tried to shake away the grogginess before replying.

"Geez, I hope Ma will just let us go right home and sleep a little instead of dragging us to Saint Michael's."

This time Jonathan looked back again as a slight smile came to his face.

"You hoping that, huh? Well, don't count on it. Best to get awake now because by 9:00 we're going to be sitting on that wooden church bench just like it was any old Sunday back before we enlisted."

Joseph shrugged.

"Yeah, I know. I'm just saying I really could use a lot more sleep. This sleeping on a train for a couple days straight ain't that easy, ya know?"

Jonathan didn't answer right away, but after a few more moments he nodded.

"Sure, but let's not complain too much, especially to Ma, right? She's going to be head over heels happy for us to be home and we don't want her to think that we're complaining about what it took for us to get here, like we would rather have not made the trip. I'm sure she knows it's not too easy to travel two thousand miles, she doesn't need to hear us complaining about it."

Jonathan's tones were congenial but Joseph immediately picked up on the command, the orders, his brother had just issued him. In their new world of the United States Army Air Forces both of them were of equal rank – corporals – and presuming they both made it through flight training, they would become Air Corps second lieutenants at the same time. Yet the old ways from home with the eldest son Jonathan clearly "outranking" his year-younger brother still held true, apparently.

Still, Joseph felt no ill will towards his brother or the presumption of a personal chain of command between the two of them. Jonathan had been a football star in high school; had lugged tens of thousands of heavy, bulky boxes of produce in the middle of the night down at the Strip District; and had gone through that tough breakup with Francine last Christmas. Joseph Coleman? Until five or six months ago he was like most other high school boys all around Pittsburgh: nobody particularly special nor with any character-forming events in his life's story thus far.

Besides, in basic training Jonathan looked out for his younger brother. When that oversized guy from Wyoming had taken a dislike to Joseph for whatever reason and began bullying the younger Coleman, Jonathan had stepped in and leveled the much-larger private once, and made it clear that the next time would go far worse for the ranch boy. So a command or two from Jonathan to his younger brother about how to behave or what to say during their too-brief days at home was certainly nothing for Joseph to think twice about.

"They'll all be there, you think, right?" Joseph asked.

Jonathan chuckled.

"You really think there's any way Ma would let any of them not be there waiting for us? Besides, you know as well as I do Thomas and Charlene and Ruthie want to see us step off the train in our uniforms."

Joseph started to say something to his brother then caught himself. Jonathan had caught the unintelligible syllable escaping from his younger brother's mouth but didn't press the matter. He knew exactly what Joseph was about to say. Maybe not the exact words, but definitely the sentiment.

What about Francine?

* * *

Francine Donner sat with her parents, her brother, and her sister halfway back from the altar at Saint Michael's. The early Sunday Mass had begun at 7:30 that morning and with the country on War Time, it wouldn't be until a quarter past eight that sunshine began to filter through the stained glass windows. She knew that mere moments from now a train would be pulling into Penn Station downtown, less than two miles away; and on that train would be the man she had hurt so deeply eleven months earlier. She was also certain that Irene Coleman would be marching Jonathan, along with the rest of her family, into Saint Michael's for the next Mass and was hopeful that encountering Jonathan this very morning as her family left and his arrived would be unavoidable.

For months now, she had waited anxiously for his return to Pittsburgh on furlough, and knew from her younger brother Louis – at fifteen, the same age as Jonathan's brother Thomas – that indeed Jonathan would be home for Thanksgiving. For almost two months after that fateful Christmas Eve the previous year, Jonathan and Francine had crossed paths rather frequently; which of course wasn't surprising considering that the Coleman and Donner houses were no more than ten minutes apart. Several times Francine had tried to engage Jonathan in conversation beyond a strained "hello" but each time

Jonathan had quietly, painfully cut off the conversation with "Not now, alright?" or a similar utterance.

Finally on a warmish Friday afternoon as the month of February headed on the downside she had succeeded in cornering him for what she hoped would be that long-delayed, apology-riddled conversation she had wanted to have since the year had begun. Jonathan had been just leaving work at *J. Weisberg & Sons*, the Strip District produce store where he had worked since graduating, right around 9:00 in the morning. Francine was there waiting for him right outside the front door of the store, still bundled up tightly in her jacket and wearing ear muffs and a scarf despite the temperature creeping above 30 degrees. This time there would be no escape for Jonathan out the back door, as she was certain he had done a few days earlier when she had been wandering inside the market waiting for him to come up from the storeroom on his way out.

"I would like to talk with you," she said sternly but – at least she hoped – somewhat affectionately when she saw him look up from counting his weekly pay as he almost ran into her walking through the market's front doors.

It seemed as if he had been just about to utter his latest chorus of "Not now, Francine" or words to that effect when he stopped in his tracks and just looked wordlessly at her, apparently resigned to allowing her to say whatever it was that had caused her to go to such lengths to confront him.

When it became apparent that Jonathan was not going to offer a "Go ahead" or "What would you like to say" or any other utterance, Francine continued.

"I want to say how very sorry I am for what happened," she said, making sure to lock eyes with him as she spoke. Francine had thought through this encounter perhaps two hundred times in her mind since late last year and had long ago come to the conclusion that downcast eyes and a shamed look on her face was not the way to go. She *would* acknowledge the terrible wrong she had done to Jonathan by having gone all the way with his best friend, but she would not offer herself up as a terrible person unworthy of the very air she breathed or the place on this earth that she occupied. She wasn't the first girl to do something so incredibly stupid like letting Donnie Yablonski manipulate and use her before he headed off to the Army. But while what she had done might have been stupid, it had not been evil. Francine might never be able to fully repair the hurt she had caused Jonathan, and their days together were apparently over forever, but she wanted to be able to finish the apology she had begun last Christmas Eve but had never completed because Jonathan had fled from her house.

"I know I hurt you terribly and I will never forgive myself for that," she continued. "I keep thinking of how stupid I was and how…"

"Enough," Jonathan interrupted, but not unkindly. He had raised his right hand in that "please stop" motion.

"It's over and done," he continued, continuing to lock eyes with her. Just as Francine was determined not to cast her eyes downward in hurtful shame, so too was Jonathan determined that he was not going to look here, there, and everywhere else to let Francine know just how painfully heartbreaking her very appearance was to him even after all these months.

"I'm not mad anymore," he continued. "I guess…"

He had paused for a long while before continuing, Francine remembered as that entire scene played in her mind as she sat in Saint Michael's this Sunday morning. Then she remembered him saying:

"I don't know, I guess that if, um, if, you know, that had happened sometime before then it would still have been, you know, painful. But finding out right when I was just starting to ask you to marry me and give you a ring..."

"I know," Francine quietly interrupted, and this time she did look downwards; terribly ashamed. She had felt her own pain for nearly two months, and supposed she could put herself in Jonathan's place and feel his own anguish. However, it wasn't until that February morning standing outside *Weisberg's* that she really felt what he had in that moment and the immediate aftermath, she realized.

They talked for a few minutes as they walked down Smallman Street a little ways before cutting up to get to Penn Avenue and the streetcar route. Jonathan was headed home, and Francine fully intended to ride with him and perhaps continue this conversation a bit longer.

Waiting at the streetcar stop, Francine finally offered what she hoped her nerves and the trajectory of this conversation would allow her to say.

But it all went horribly wrong.

"I hear you're leaving for Air Corps training in June with Joseph," she said quietly; sadly.

He nodded and also seemed to have a somber look on his face as he did; at least that's what Francine thought.

"Maybe before you leave we could, you know, go out for dinner one night..."

Somberness turned to cold bitterness in a flash as Jonathan cut her off.

"Why? So you can say goodbye to me just like you said goodbye to Donnie?"

What Francine remembered all these months since that February morning – and which was part of the reason she was sitting here in Saint Michael's this November Sunday morning so anxiously hoping that she would encounter Jonathan – was that even before he finished his single nasty utterance that icy, disdainful look that had so suddenly appeared on his face had vanished just as quickly. Francine could almost see Jonathan's brain struggling to recall the first few words he had just spoken, or at least not continue on. But as Francine knew from several occasions in her own life, sometimes one's mouth has a mind of its own and once a sentiment begins to pour forth, there will be no halting the path to its conclusion.

What Francine also recalled about that day was that as the icy glare disappeared from Jonathan's face that same look no doubt immediately came to her own as his final syllable was being uttered. She could feel her own eyes narrow at him, her cheekbones almost hurting; feel the disdain radiating forth from her at what he had just said.

She had clenched her teeth, spun, and wordlessly walked away in the other direction as she could hear Jonathan's voice becoming fainter with each step: "Francine...Francine... I'm sorry, I didn't mean to say that. I'm sorry..."

* * *

Jonathan began gathering his duffel bag as the train slowly chugged to a stop. At that very same moment he was also thinking about that encounter with Francine back in February. For months he had figuratively kicked himself for what he had said. Not so much for the words or the sentiments themselves; as far as he had been concerned, they were perfectly justified considering what Francine had done with Donnie.   But the intervening months while at Thunderbird Field had mellowed his righteous indignation somewhat as he came to realize that from the moment the bombs began falling on Pearl Harbor, these were not ordinary times. People were doing strange things, and more than a few of his new comrades in arms at basic training told tales similar to his as the new airmen got to know each other. And surprisingly, at least half of them told their new buddies that after digesting it all, they were still planning on marrying that girl back home, indiscretions and all, if she wasn't yet taken when they made it back on furlough. But in the meantime, they would see if they could wrangle any Arizona cowgirls while out at Thunderbird Field; a bit of turnabout to even the score, some of these Air Corps boys seemed to feel…

What bothered Jonathan throughout his remaining time in Pittsburgh that winter and spring of '42 before heading west, and what still bothered him, was having given Francine a sort of moral high ground thanks to the sheer viciousness of what he had blurted out at her. He knew she felt very badly about what she had done with Donnie; knew that she had been drunker than she had ever been in her life that night, thanks to Donnie pouring one drink after another in her at the Crawford Grille until getting her back to the hotel room at the William Penn. Francine was partly to blame for putting herself in that position, he still felt, but the lion's share of the fault lay with Donnie Yablonski, not Francine Donner.

If Jonathan hadn't blurted out those brutal, spiteful words in response to Francine's overture then quite possibly he might have found himself forgiving and forgetting over the following months – well, maybe not forgetting, though he would certainly try – what had happened between Donnie and Francine. Over time, perhaps, he and Francine might actually get back together, or at least try to. He had learned to force away those terrible images of the two of them in that hotel room bed…

He quickly shook his head again to force the thoughts away as he was gathering his belongings and this time his brother noticed.

"What's wrong?" Joseph asked. "You got a headache or something?"

Jonathan, unaware that he had physically tried to shake that persistent, terrible vision of the two of them out of his thoughts, looked over at his brother.

"Nah, not really," he said quietly before willing his mood to brighten.

"Come on, let's go see the folks," he told his brother, noting that Joseph's weariness seemed to have given way to the excitement of the homecoming.

As Joseph eased his way into the flow of soldiers and sailors shuffling their way off the train, leaving behind others who would continue onwards to Harrisburg or Philadelphia or perhaps some small town stop on their way to their own Thanksgiving furloughs, Jonathan reached down into the left pocket of his uniform pants, underneath his handkerchief, and as he did dozens of times each day, made sure that the Morgan dollar was still there. That special Christmas gift from his father nearly a year ago; the 1891 silver coin, no longer minted, that Jonathan's grandfather had given Gerald Coleman just before Gerald shipped out for Europe and the Great War.

That talisman that Gerald had all but promised would keep Jonathan safe and bring him just enough luck and protection when he would need it the most.

Satisfied that the Morgan silver dollar was safely resting at the bottom of his pocket, Jonathan thought to himself as he followed his brother into the aisle that indeed the allegedly charmed coin's powers may well be needed during this furlough if he encountered Francine Donner.

Which, he admitted to himself, was what he wanted to happen after all.

* * *

Irene Coleman spotted her boys on the train platform before anyone else in the family, as expected. Her first instinct was to raise her right hand that wasn't clutching her pocketbook and to wave wildly until Jonathan and Joseph spotted her. But something about seeing her sons wearing their Army Air Forces uniforms for the very first time caused her to instead bring that hand to her mouth, almost as if for the very first time she was forced to acknowledge that her little boys had indeed become military men. She felt the moistness come to her eyes but willed the tears to stop before they really got going. There would be no crying; at least not now.

So it was Charlene who spotted her brothers and excitedly called out to them.

"Here! Over here! Jonathan! Joey! Over here!"

Joseph picked up the faint sound of his sister's voice over the racket on the crowded platform that was getting louder as one family reunion was followed by another and then another, almost by the second. He looked in the direction that he thought Charlene's voice was coming from and then after spotting her – as well as his parents – he nudged Jonathan and then nodded in the direction they needed to head.

The Coleman brothers wove their way through the crowd, brushing up against and squeezing through numerous other Pittsburghers, until they reached their awaiting family. The next couple of minutes were a flurry of hugs and kisses and handshakes – including many repeats, since Irene hugged each of her sons at least three times each during the extended greeting – combined with one unfinished, interrupted partial sentence after another:

"I'm so glad you're home, we've been…"

"How was the train trip? Did you…"

"No, we only got off the train a couple times when we were changing railroads in Oklahoma and then later in…"

"Did you get all the letters I wrote? Did you see that I wrote you about…"

When the frenzy finally subsided, and the crowd had begun to disperse a bit as families walked away together from the platform and out of Penn Station to wherever they might be headed this Sunday, the Colemans finally had a bit of space around them along with some relative quiet.

"Are you boys ready to go to Saint Michael's?" Irene asked.

Jonathan looked out of the corner of his eyes to his left at his younger brother, hoping that his earlier warning to Joseph was still in the younger brother's thoughts.

"Yep; let's go," was all Joseph said.

*   *   *

All the way up the aisle through the back half of Saint Michael's, Francine walked proudly, her head up, her eyes scanning the faces of the many young men in uniform who were heading into the church for the next Mass.

Nothing.

The entire time Francine was walking with her family away from Saint Michael's after the conclusion of the morning Mass she kept looking back over her shoulder at other arrivals. She was almost ready to turn the corner at the next intersection, maybe fifty yards away from the church, when she spotted him. She wasn't fully certain at first because of the tan service cap covering the top part of that particular young man's head, and because his face was angled away from Francine as he walked towards Saint Michael's. But there was another uniformed boy with him whom she was fairly certain was his brother Joseph. Then she recognized Gerald and Irene Coleman, and Charlene also, trailing a few steps behind, and then she knew.

She immediately wished she had dawdled three or four minutes inside the church – that would have been enough – and for an instant thought about concocting some pretense to her parents to quickly walk back to Saint Michael's. But by then Jonathan would almost certainly have already been seated with his family, not to mention Francine's own parents would have immediately become suspicious.

She dismissed the idea, disappointed that at least for this Sunday morning there would be coming face to face with Jonathan Coleman for Francine.

But there was always later today…and then tomorrow…and then…

* * *

"I'd like all the young men present in a military uniform to please stand for a moment," Father Nolan said about two-thirds of the way through the service, immediately after concluding his homily. After a moment's hesitation both Jonathan and Joseph stood, along with perhaps four dozen others scattered throughout all corners of the congregation.

Joseph in particular, but his brother as well, was particularly thankful for this unanticipated interlude. During the twenty-five minutes it took Father Nolan to deliver his extra-long homily this morning, Joseph caught himself just as he dozed off at least five times, and his brother Thomas nudged him three additional times after seeing Joseph's head begin to slowly drop. Jonathan was a little more awake, but not much; his father sharply elbowed his oldest son twice to likewise keep him from nodding off.

"These brave young men standing in our midst are our future and also our present," Father Nolan said. "They are all embarking on a mission of freedom for…"

As Father Nolan spoke Joseph Coleman, thankful for at least a minute or two of respite from fighting off desperately needed sleep by virtue of having to stand, found his eyes scanning backs of heads and side views of faces of others standing within his field of vision, and twice turning his head to look at some of the other young men in uniform. Almost every face was at least somewhat familiar, and he reckoned that more than half of them were friends of his, most of them graduates within the past two or three years from Schenley High School. Joseph found his thoughts time-traveling as his mind placed a story or two with almost every face.

Tommy Bonnaverte, over there in the Navy uniform; that showdown schoolyard fight between the two of them in sixth grade which had ended in a draw, after which Tommy and Joseph became best of friends for the next three years.

Stan Greenfield, one of the many Jews at Schenley who mixed easily with the Poles, Italians, and the Black kids. His slightly chubby boyish face was now lean and hardened, and how odd he looked wearing a crisp Marine uniform!

Walter Dennison, who carried the nickname "Wrong Way" throughout his latter years in high school after the infamous "Wrong Way" Riegels who had run the wrong way on the football field back in the '29 Rose Bowl. Dennison had started to do the same thing against Westinghouse two seasons earlier after intercepting a pass and becoming disoriented as he wildly avoided two Westinghouse would-be tacklers. Fortunately Walt's mistake was only for about twenty yards and at mid-field before too much damage could be done. As it turned out the speedy Jonathan Coleman caught up with Dennison, spun him around, and actually led Walt all the way back down through the Westinghouse team to score a touchdown with Joseph and the rest of the Schenley team cheering wildly at this amazing sight. But here was Walt Dennison, wearing an Army Air Forces cadet uniform just as Joseph and Jonathan were. Joseph had an immediate flash of another famous person nicknamed "Wrong Way" – the aviator Corrigan, who claimed he flew from New York to Ireland "accidentally" back in '38 instead of the other direction to California – and instantly had the terrible image of Walter Dennison getting separated from his squadron and lost one day up in the sky after getting his wings, and then flying straight into Germany and a fiery death at the hands of Nazi Messerschmitts instead of back to safety in England.

Joseph looked over at his older brother and saw that Jonathan's eyes were also scanning the crowd, and presumed the brothers' thoughts at the moment were one and the same as his own.

* * *

Sunday's dinner at the Coleman home after returning from Mass was indeed worthy of been served four days hence for Thanksgiving. Not just the roast beef, ham, beans, turnips, carrots, potatoes, home-baked breads, pies and cakes, and all the rest of the exquisitely delicious food prepared by Irene and her sister-in-law Lois Walker along with Charlene and her cousin Lorraine.

The company. The wondrous atmosphere of family togetherness that had been absent from the Coleman and Walker households since Jonathan, Joseph, and Marty had sadly departed months earlier, even though only two of the three were present this Sunday afternoon. The many stories and anecdotes of the past six months, some of which had already been related in letters but needed to be retold, while others freshly new.

They all seemed to steer the conversation away from news of the war fronts, though the news related by that day's *Pittsburgh Press* in the headline that read "Allies Pound Axis Lines in Tunisia; Foes Brace for Last-Ditch Stands" did bear some discussion given that Marty Walker's *U.S.S. Augusta* had played a role in the early stages of the North Africa invasion. But for the most part, discussion was about *anything* except the war news.

"Ready to tell them?" Joseph Coleman said to his brother all of a sudden as second helpings of pie and cake were passed around to everyone seated at the table – including seven-year old Ruth – even though nearly everyone was slumped back, clearly fuller from this meal than they had been from any other in recent memory.

Sharp looks of concern from Irene and Lois Walker; raised eyebrows from Gerald Coleman. Joseph caught the looks on his parents' and aunt's faces.

"Oh no," he said quickly, "Nothing bad. Jonathan and I have some news that we didn't write about in any of our letters since we wanted to save it for when we got home on furlough."

The concerned looks all turned to puzzlement.

"Sure, go ahead," Jonathan replied to his brother who barely let a breath slip by between the last syllable of Jonathan's short statement of approval and the delivery of his news.

"Jonathan and I are in a movie, and it's in the theaters right now!" he exclaimed, now totally unable to contain his excitement.

"A movie?" Irene Coleman looked over at her son.

"Uh-huh," Joseph continued. "*Thunder Birds*, they filmed most of it at Thunderbird Field back in the spring before we got there but they came back in July to do some retakes. They had a bunch of us cadets doing marching and took some movies of us doing calisthenics and the obstacle course, and used the scenes in the movie!"

"They had a special showing at the air field last month when it came out," Jonathan chimed in, "and there we were, Joseph and I, in at least two scenes that we could tell. In one we were…"

Joseph interrupted.

"We want to go see it while we're home, they would only show it to us one time out there and we never got an off-base pass between when the movie came out and when we just came home."

"You were in a movie?" Ruthie suddenly asked, apparently grasping what the discussion was about.

"Uh-huh," Jonathan said tenderly. "If you go to the movies you can see Joseph and me up there" – he pointed upward towards an imaginary movie screen – "bigger than you can imagine."

"Did you meet Mickey Mouse when you made the movie?" she asked, apparently falling back on her frame of reference that all movies had to have Mickey Mouse…especially *Fantasia*, which her mother had taken her to see over at the Strand almost a dozen times in the two years since its release.

Laughter all around the table as Jonathan answered.

"No, we didn't get to meet Mickey Mouse," he said.

Joseph chimed in.

"But we did get to meet Gene…"

Charlene gasped, an act noticed immediately by her cousin Lorraine across the table…as well as Charlene's mother.

"…Tierney," Joseph continued, oblivious to his sister's involuntary utterance, referring to the movie's female lead actress, the gorgeous brunette who had just begun to make a name for herself in Hollywood.

The conversation shifted to the minutest details of the Coleman brothers' cameo appearance in an actual Hollywood movie that was showing right now over at the Senator down near Pennsylvania Station – one starring Preston Foster and Gene Tierney, nonetheless! – and then onto new movies in general; the Pittsburgh Pirates' abysmal performance in the recently concluded baseball season; the latest rationing measures; and most anything else that the Colemans and Walkers could think of to discuss.

One might have thought, listening to the dinner table conversation go on for almost three more hours with new helpings of food and dessert making their way to the table periodically along the way and new discussion topics springing to life when the conversation seemed to have finally died, that none of them wanted the occasion of this gathering to ever end.

* * *

There was no Sunday supper at the Coleman house that evening, at least not in a formal, sitting-at-the-table sense. Enough food had been consumed by one and all to have constituted three, perhaps four normal meals. Even compared to pre-war, pre-rationing days, the bounty would have been considered extraordinary; a once-every-few-years extravaganza, reserved for only the most extra-special of holiday occasions. In fact the food served during the many Thanksgiving and Christmas dinners during the long, lean Depression years had been carefully meted out by Irene Coleman and Lois Walker to their families on each occasion, though the women did their best to make the meals on each of those feasts as plentiful as could possibly be mustered. The closest anyone could remember to this Sunday's extravagant, hours-long banquet was the previous year's Thanksgiving, with the Depression years mostly behind them all and the sudden attack on Pearl Harbor still a week and a half away. Today topped even that day, though; and more than one of the quietly belching "survivors" of the meal wondered just how the coming Thursday's actual Thanksgiving meal could possibly top what had just been experienced.

After the Colemans and Walkers began to filter away from the table, the women and girls headed to the smallish kitchen to put away the leftovers, wash the many dishes, and finish cleaning up. As tired as Joseph and Jonathan were, still sleep-deprived from their long cross-country train travel, they resisted the urge to head to their rooms – though technically now their old rooms, given that both had become military men – to catch an hour or two of much-needed sleep.

Instead, they parked themselves in the living room with their father, their brother Thomas, and their uncle Stan. Joseph, sitting next to the radio, twirled through the Philco's dial to pick up the NBC Red Network. Jack Benny would be on in a couple hours, at 7:00, so until then they just kept the radio at a lowered volume.

The discuss-anything conversation from the dinner table spilled over into the living room, and Stan Walker filled the Coleman boys in on everything he could possibly remember to tell them about their cousin Marty. At Thunderbird Field Jonathan and Joseph had closely followed the invasion of North Africa through the first days of November. Stan Walker remarked that he would have thought the specific presence of the *U.S.S. Augusta* by name would have been censored from news reports coming back from North Africa, but apparently Patton's and Eisenhower's press officers must have wanted it known that the very cruiser on which President Roosevelt had met Churchill back in the summer of '41, before America had entered the war, was playing a key part in the combined efforts of the U.S. and the British to smash the Nazis. Thus Stan knew that his son had taken part in this massive effort, though of course he did not know the specific role Marty had played...or, for a fact, if Marty was still safe at this moment.

Just before 6:30 Lois Walker appeared in the living room, Lorraine at her side. Both mother and daughter looked totally exhausted from the massive cleanup effort they had undertaken for almost two hours. Stan stood up; all three of the Walkers said their goodnights and thank-yous to Gerald, Irene, and everyone; and then Stan's family departed.

Her houseguests now departed, Irene walked into the living room, one of the good China dishes in one hand and a dish rag in the other at work drying the plate, and asked Jonathan and Joseph in particular but also her husband and her youngest son,

"Are you hungry?"

Four sets of cheeks bulged simultaneously at the very idea of more food.

"No thanks, Ma," Jonathan spoke up first. "That was fantastic, I don't think I'll be able to eat the entire rest of the week until Thanksgiving."

"Me too," Joseph added.

"Well, maybe later on," Irene countered before heading back into the kitchen, determined that her Army sons would want for nothing while they were home.

"Better than Army food, huh?" Gerald said after Irene was out of sight.

Both boys chucked at the same time.

"That's for sure," Joseph said. "Mostly they give us a whole lot of S.O.S..." – he caught himself uttering the off-color acronym – "...I mean, creamed chipped beef, that sort of thing. Can't say that the food at Thunderbird is anything to write home about."

"And that's why we haven't written home about it," Jonathan added. His father looked over at his eldest son, surprised. Jonathan had always been studious; serious; and, for the six months before he left for Phoenix very somber, no doubt because of that business with Francine. Gerald Coleman hadn't heard his son joking around for...well, for a long while, and then only occasionally. But since his arrival this morning he had been almost jovial; definitely out of character but nothing that would cause Gerald any worry, of course. He had actually worried that some aftermath of that business with Francine might overshadow this visit; that perhaps Jonathan's mood would darken by returning home to the city where that girl still was, despite the holiday.

Gerald had fully expected Francine Donner to somehow find a way to cross paths with Jonathan this morning at Saint Michael's. He didn't hold anything against the girl; she had made a terrible mistake with the other boy and had wounded Jonathan in the process, but Gerald had always liked her. Still, this visit was so important to all of them, Irene in particular, that a moody Jonathan pining for his old girlfriend was the last thing Gerald wanted to happen. And fortunately, at least so far, it seemed that would not be the case.

Joseph was…well, much the same, Gerald thought. At least he wasn't walking around shooting off his mouth about joining up to kill Germans and Japs the way he had been for months after Pearl Harbor. No doubt the gravity of what he would soon face had been driven home to him out there in Arizona, and the boy clearly and fully understood that he was not headed off to "play war" but in fact would wind up putting his life on the line.

Gerald's concern of the moment was, surprisingly, not about either of his Air Corps sons but rather his other boy, Thomas. This morning at Penn Station and then during the streetcar ride up to Saint Michael's, from the moment Jonathan and Joseph came into view and hurried over to greet their family, Thomas had been unnaturally quiet. During the hours-long meal, Thomas had also said very little. Several times Gerald looked surreptitiously at Thomas while they had been gathered at the table, and each time he seemed to be looking uneasily at one or the other of his older brothers.

The boy was fifteen now, Gerald thought as he watched Jonathan get up out of his chair and walk over to the radio to turn up the volume since Jack Benny was about to start. He quickly directed his eyes to Thomas, and sure enough the boy seemed to be uncomfortably staring at Jonathan. So quite possibly the shock of seeing his older brothers in uniform was bringing home to Thomas that very likely he himself would be wearing a military uniform of his own before this war was settled one way or another, and the very thought petrified him as the war news, day by day, screamed their headlines of major battles and killings by the thousands.

*   *   *

Gerald Coleman was partly correct about what was bothering Thomas. Upon seeing his brothers in uniform this morning he did indeed project his own life three years into the future or so and involuntarily saw visions of his slightly older self fighting Nazis all across North Africa, or being with the Marines and trying to survive the day-by-day horror on Guadalcanal only to wonder if he indeed did survive if that next island would then be the one where they would finally get him.

More than that, though, was that the sight of Jonathan and Joseph in their Army Air Forces uniforms brought home to Thomas that the natural, age-based rhythm between the two oldest boys and him was now a gaping chasm. He had always been "the youngest" or "little Coleman" or simply "their little brother." But for the most part, neighbors and family members usually thought of Jonathan, Joseph, and Thomas as a triumvirate of sorts. All three played football at Schenley and now that Thomas was a sophomore he had made the varsity team this past fall and, most would agree, was already a better player than Joseph had been at any point. Likewise, for more than five years all three had played baseball together in the sandlots in and around the Oakland section of Pittsburgh, and more often than not the batting order would be one Coleman after another in the 2nd, 3rd, and 4th positions: speedy

Thomas, then Joseph, and then the slugging Jonathan hitting in the cleanup position.

Now, though, anyone in Polish Hill or Oakland or anywhere else around Pittsburgh might look at the three of them walking in to the Senator to watch *Thunder Birds*, or seated at the Sun Drugs counter having burgers and shakes, or doing most any other thing the three of them might do sometime later this week and think of the uniformed Jonathan and Joseph as men; as comrades in arms...with their pesky younger brother just tagging along, no doubt because they were "letting him."

Worse, Thomas' older brothers now shared almost six months of Air Corps training far away in Arizona, living and training together day after day after day. Thomas not only wasn't out there with them, he had only the vaguest ideas of what his big brothers experienced by virtue of movies he had seen at the Schenley or the Strand or the Senator that depicted military training life in one way or another. Other people's perceptions were one thing; the sad reality was that there now really *was* now a significant difference between Thomas and his older brothers, and the gap could only continue to grow.

Thomas wasn't aware of the sadness creeping into his face as he sat there with his father and his brothers listening to Jack Benny and *The Grape Nuts Program* and then Kay Kyser and even all of *The Chase and Sanborn Hour* until Jonathan and Joseph both stood in unison at 8:30 just as Edgar Bergen signed off.

"Pop, we have to get some sleep," Jonathan offered on behalf of his brother as well.

"We're totally worn out from the train ride and..."

Gerald interrupted by holding up his right hand.

"It's fine, I know how tired you boys are," he answered. "You both go get some shuteye and you'll be all fresh in the morning."

The four Colemans said their goodnights to one another, leaving Thomas behind with his father. As *One Man's Family* began Gerald looked over at his youngest son's morose face. He stood, walked over to the Philco, and turned the volume back down to barely above a whisper.

"What's on your mind, Tommy?"

Thomas looked up at his father.

"Nothing."

Gerald just stood there by the radio, looking back his son; that look that demanded an answer sooner or later without having to use any further words. Still, Thomas stubbornly refused to verbalize what he was thinking.

Gerald walked over to the sofa next to his son, sat down, put his right hand on Thomas' left knee gently but firmly, and looked his son squarely in the eyes.

"What's on your mind?" he repeated, and this time the command would not be denied.

Thomas tried to tell his father what he had been thinking – what he had been feeling – as best he could.

*   *   *

Irene Coleman stood in her kitchen, a cup of coffee in her right hand and what she intended to be her final Pall Mall of the evening in her left. Jonathan and Joseph had already gone off to bed in their old rooms but she fully expected her husband and the others in the family to finally be hungry for more food before too long. And so, as she would do most any day, she waited in her kitchen.

While she waited, Irene Coleman also thought over and over and over about Charlene's inadvertent gasp during the Sunday dinner. The moment had passed apparently unnoticed by almost everyone else, though Irene did catch Charlene and Lorraine exchange lightning-quick glances across the table at each other before looking away.

No doubt this was about a new boyfriend named "Gene" – Irene had certainly made note of the words spoken just before Charlene's gasp, and Joseph had been talking about that actress who spelled her name as a man might do. Irene thought back to a few days before the previous Christmas when Lorraine had been party to Charlene's little secret engagement to Larry Moncheck that, fortunately, was now a distant memory. The two girls were thick as thieves most of the time, which is what would be expected from girl cousins of their ages who had been so close to each other for years.

But there was something more, Irene thought to herself as she took a deep drag on the Pall Mall, her mind grasping for...well, something it couldn't quite reach. Charlene had had at least three boyfriends since last Valentine's Day when she had broken up with Larry for good, apparently coming to grips that a so-called engagement without any sort of ring wasn't really an engagement at all despite what the boy had told her; and none of those boys had been kept a secret from Irene. In fact each time Charlene seemed to have gone out of her way to mention the new boy's name a dozen time for several days in the presence of her mother, as if she were especially proud to have landed herself a new suitor. And of course from the very beginning each of those boys had come to the Coleman house to pick up Francine for weekend dates and persevered through the obligatory encounters with not only Irene but also Charlene's father before being allowed to head off to the movies or roller rink or wherever they might be going.

After Larry had vanished Charlene had immediately started dating Henry Solomon and even though Irene felt uneasy that her daughter was seeing a Jewish boy, he had seemed nice enough and Irene was actually a little bit sorry when Henry and Charlene called it quits just before the end of the school year. Then over the summer there had been that one Oakland boy Bobby Duncan, and then at the beginning of Charlene's senior year she began going out with Lee Svetnic. Irene had never heard officially that Charlene was through with Lee but he hadn't come calling since the week after Schenley's homecoming game, so Irene presumed that that relationship was now also concluded.

This time though…well, there was *something* because of how the girls had reacted to that name. Well, no matter, Irene thought to herself as she crushed out the Pall Mall at the sound of approaching footsteps as Gerald and Thomas walked towards the kitchen, apparently finally hungry enough to seek out more food. She would find out what Charlene was hiding…and, more importantly, the reason for the secrecy.

2 – Monday, November 23, 1942

The alarm bell took almost a minute to penetrate Jonathan's deep sleep; which wasn't surprising since he had just enjoyed the most wonderful night of sleep in...well, perhaps his whole life, at least that's how he felt as his mind swam upwards into the morning.

He had slept nearly eleven hours straight – dropping off within seconds shortly before 8:45 the previous night and awakening to the alarm clock he had set for 7:30. No doubt he could have slept for hours longer but he knew his furlough time was limited, and he was determined not to sleep the entire time away. Besides, his Pa would be home only until 8:00 that morning before leaving for his supervisor's job at the war plant up on Mount Washington that made Army boots and shoes. Ordinarily Gerald was at work by 7:30 every morning but knowing that his sons would want to sleep in at least a little bit this first morning of their furlough, and wanting to be at the breakfast table when they came down to Irene's kitchen, he had asked for and received permission to come in at 8:30 and in exchange work an extra hour that evening.

Jonathan sat up in his bed, leaned forward to put his face in his hands as his elbows rested on his knees, and brought his mind into focus along with his vision. A minute or so later he left his room and walked next door to Joseph's. His brother was still lost to the world, lightly snoring away.

"Corporal!" Jonathan barked from the doorway, mustering the classic drill sergeant tones. "Ten-hut!"

Joseph jolted awake and within two seconds was on his feet standing by the side of his bed, struggling to come to attention when he realized where he was. He looked over at his older brother, standing in the doorway smirking.

"Jerk!" Joseph growled as he slumped back onto his bed, oozing himself prone once again.

"Come on," Jonathan said in his normal voice this time. "Get up, let's go get some breakfast."

"I'm still dog-tired," Joseph grunted. "I'm going back to sleep."

"Come on," Jonathan said again, this time his tones halfway between normal and mock drill sergeant. "I'm beat too but once we're down at breakfast we'll be wide awake before you know it. Pop should still be there for a little bit longer, and Ma doesn't want us sleeping the whole day away, you know?"

Joseph rolled his eyes.

"Yeah, I know," he said. "Gimme a minute, okay?"

Jonathan nodded.

"Sure," he replied and turned to leave Joseph's room but then turned back towards his brother.

"Make it two minutes and be downstairs in five, okay?" This second "okay" from Jonathan, though, could more accurately be translated to something along the lines of "over and out;" an unmistakable command.

"Yeah, okay," Joseph groaned as he pulled his pillow on top of his face.

*   *   *

Irene Coleman had already begun piling the hotcakes on her sons' plates as she heard the first heavy footsteps coming from the top of the stairs. A moment later Jonathan appeared in the kitchen doorway and marched straight in to give Irene a kiss on her cheek.

"Morning, Ma," he said and then walked over to the kitchen table where Gerald had just laid down the morning *Post-Gazette*. "Morning, Pa," Jonathan said, resting his right hand lightly and briefly on his father's right shoulder; that was about as affectionate as any of the Coleman men had ever gotten with each other, and six months away at Army Air Forces training did nothing to change that.

"Joseph will be right down," he said as he slid into the chair to the right of his father as Irene placed a large stack of steaming hotcakes in front of her oldest son.

"Go ahead and start," she said but Irene needn't have said anything; Jonathan was already digging in for the first bite even as his left hand was reaching for the maple syrup in the middle of the table.

"How did you sleep?" Gerald asked.

Jonathan grinned.

"*Almost* as comfortable as the barracks," he joked. "Not quite, but *almost*."

Gerald smiled back.

"I'll bet," he said.

Almost a full minute of silence followed as Jonathan gulped one healthy mouthful of hotcakes after another, his fork never coming to rest in between bites.

"In a hurry?" Gerald asked, taking note of the speed at which his son was wolfing down his breakfast.

For a moment Jonathan was puzzled by the question, then realized why his father had asked him that. He rested his fork on his plate and reached for his coffee, which he had yet to touch.

"You know, I didn't even realize I was eating that fast. I guess I've just gotten used to eating in the chow hall three meals a day and especially when you're near the end of the line, you sometimes only have a couple minutes to eat before they yell at us to get back outside in formation."

"Well, try to take it easy while you're home," Gerald said. "I noticed you were eating fast at the table yesterday but figured that was because you hadn't had a good meal in a couple days while you boys were on the train, and were extra hungry."

"There's plenty more," Irene chimed in. "No need for you to rush or worry about not getting enough to eat."

"That's for sure," Jonathan said as he watched his mother place another stack of hotcakes on his plate just as Joseph made his entrance into the kitchen.

"Morning, Ma," he said as he repeated what his brother had done a few moments earlier, first kissing his mother on her cheek and then walking over to pat his father on his shoulder before sitting down on the other side of Gerald. Irene was just setting down the plate of hotcakes in front of Joseph when Jonathan looked across the table at his brother and said,

"Don't eat real fast like we do in the chow hall; Pop just noticed that I was doing that."

It took Joseph a few seconds to fully understand his brother.

"Yeah, I got you," he answered. "Good thing you said something, I woulda finished this whole stack in something like thirty seconds."

The Coleman boys did their best to eat deliberately and slowly to enjoy the home-cooked breakfast their mother had prepared for them, grateful for having more than five or ten minutes seated at a table for the first time in months. Gazing over at the morning *Post-Gazette*, Jonathan reached for the paper that was top-down, flipped it over, and took in the headline.

ALLIES SMASH PANZER FORCE

Russians Gain 50 Miles, Kill 50,000 Nazis

"You see this?" Jonathan handed the newspaper to his brother across the table. Joseph took in the headline.

"Yeah," he said then handed the paper back to Jonathan.

"Maybe the Russkies will finish them off before we get over there, huh?" Joseph added, not believing his own words but rather parroting what the cadets back at Thunderbird Field said almost every morning among themselves when briefed on the latest war news, though also not putting any stock whatsoever in their own hopeful utterances.

Jonathan just shrugged.

"Maybe," he said as he flipped the paper over to the bottom half of the front page.

"Hey Pa, you see *this?*" he said as his eyes landed on a story near the bottom with the headline "Rescue of

Rickenbacker and Crew Reveals Saga of Real Heroism." The famous World War I ace, Eddie Rickenbacker, had been on an inspection trip for the Secretary of War when the Army plane in which he was a passenger ran out of fuel and crashed into the South Pacific.

Jonathan scanned the article quickly before handing the paper to his father. Rickenbacker and several others had been adrift in life rafts for more than three weeks before being rescued.

"I read that this morning," Gerald said but still took the paper from Jonathan. The reason Jonathan made special mention of this news report to his father was that back in the Great War during the time Gerald was a member of the American Expeditionary Forces, he had once ridden with Rickenbacker – already a hero – in the ace's biplane to personally deliver a top secret communiqué to a battalion commander who reported directly to the Allied Commander, General Pershing himself. While Gerald had never come face to the face with the famous Black Jack Pershing, he had spent nearly a full day in the company of the equally famous Rickenbacker. While his sons were growing up Gerald occasionally told them the story of that day. Now that his boys were soon to be Army pilots themselves, presuming they both passed through the rest of their flight training, his own experiences with Captain Rickenbacker seemed to take on a different significance as he looked back.

The arrival of Charlene, dressed for school, interrupted the discussion about Rickenbacker's rescue and the rest of the morning's news.

Irene made sure she was extra-pleasant to her daughter this morning when serving Charlene her plate of hot cakes; making idle conversation with Charlene while Gerald and his sons continued to talk about Eddie Rickenbacker, the war news, and other topics; and then seeing Charlene out the front door on her way to school for the day. As part of the war effort and cost-saving measures on heat, the school district had declared that this Monday's classes would be the only ones held this week, giving the students an extra-long Thanksgiving break. Charlene, Thomas, and Ruthie only had to bear one more day of classes and then the rest of the week was theirs. Plans had already been made for family events throughout the week – seeing the war movie the boys were in, going for ice cream at Isaly's since Jonathan and Joseph had been away during the entire summer, and the like – but Charlene would also have time for her own activities such as continued rehearsals through the early part of the week for the upcoming All-City High School War Bond Benefit.

Today, though, was a school day and Irene had plans for while her daughter was attending classes over at Schenley High.

While Irene was seeing Charlene and Thomas to the door before she bundled herself and Ruthie up for the morning walk to her elementary school, Gerald leaned forward and caught the attention of his two older sons.

"Boys," he said in quiet tones, "I want you to do something for me later today."

* * *

The older boys, after hearing what their father wanted them to do after Thomas was done with school this afternoon, shifted around what they had planned to do today. In fact this very morning they were headed over to

Schenley in their uniforms to visit some of their old teachers. No doubt a few other recent Schenley graduates home on furlough would be doing the same and it was expected that this Monday would be a homecoming of sorts, at least for those boys who would soon be off to one war front or another.

By 9:30 most everyone had departed the Coleman house, except for Jonathan and Joseph who would leave for the trolley stop twenty minutes later. Irene finished cleaning the morning's breakfast plates and cooking skillets, smoking one Pall Mall then another while she worked, and thinking. By 10:00, satisfied that nobody would be coming home, she went up to Charlene's room.

Irene surveyed the room – Charlene's bed, the dresser, the nightstand – before deciding where she would look first. She headed straight for the nightstand and opened the top drawer. Underneath a few jewelry trinkets was an issue of *Look* from 1941, several months before America joined the war; the cover showing a pilot standing in the cockpit of an Army Air Forces P-40 pursuit plane.

An odd item for Charlene, Irene immediately thought; far more suited for being seen resting in Joseph's nightstand drawer. Irene had a vague recollection of having seen this issue downstairs in the Coleman house at some point in the previous year, but then again for several years now so many issues of not only *Look* but also *Life* had some sort of military-themed cover photograph, and they all blended together in Irene's mind. Irene gingerly lifted the magazine out of the drawer, paying careful attention to the layout and positioning of each piece of jewelry resting on top of the glossy for when she would replace the magazine.

She held the magazine for a brief moment and then thumbed through it. As she did a small piece of stiff paper or maybe cardboard came loose and floated to the floor, tumbling several times on its way down. Irene reached down to pick it up and, since the blank back of what looked to be a calling card was facing upwards, she flipped it over to read what was on the other side:

Gene Kelly
Metro-Goldwyn-Mayer Pictures
Los Angeles, California

Underneath the printing was what appeared to be a telephone number handwritten in blue ink.

Irene's heart began racing as she stared at the calling card for almost a minute then began going through the issue of *Look* once again, this time turning the pages very slowly. She soon found what she was looking for: a photo layout of this Gene Kelly, whoever he was, with his new bride; someone named Betsy Blair, apparently an actress. Still puzzled, Irene began skimming the captions and accompanying text when suddenly "Pittsburgh, Pennsylvania" jumped out at her.

The tumblers clicked into place. This Gene Kelly character – apparently a Broadway performer – was from Pittsburgh and somewhere, somehow, he had met Charlene and given her his calling card. Why? Irene didn't yet know…but she *would* find out.

Irene replaced the calling card into the magazine – hopefully it had been in between two of the pages about this Mister Kelly, at least that was where the card was going to be placed – and then carefully laid the magazine back into Charlene's drawer. Then she arranged the jewelry on top the way she remembered it had all been laid. Irene wondered if Charlene had deliberately placed those pieces there to perhaps catch her mother prying, but wasn't certain. It didn't matter, though; quickly enough, as soon as Irene figured out the final pieces to this puzzle, she would confront her daughter and demand to know why the calling card of some actor from Metro-Goldwyn-Mayer Pictures with a hand-written telephone number was in her possession!

Suddenly Irene realized that the article had referred to this Gene Kelly as a Broadway performer; not a movie actor. Yet his card had indeed said he was with Metro-Goldwyn-Mayer Pictures. There was certainly a missing link; perhaps more than one. But then again, that issue of *Look* was more than one year old, from September of '41, so possibly Mister Kelly had joined the movies since the article was printed.

Plus the main theme of the article, as well as the pictures, were of Mister Kelly and his new wife, this Betsy Blair. Why would a newly married man be giving his card to a young girl anyway, whether or not he himself was from Pittsburgh?

No matter; Irene would learn the full story soon enough.

* * *

Gerald Coleman had a great deal of difficulty keeping his mind on his job this morning. Just as Charlene, Thomas, and Ruth would be done with school for the week after this afternoon, so too would Gerald be done with work. However, unlike his children's schools, the army shoe plant was not closing for the week. In contrast, it would continue to run the entire week except for Thanksgiving Day. However, with his sons at home, Gerald had made arrangements to trade shifts with the man who ran the weekend afternoon shifts. He would go into work on Friday, after his sons had left from Penn Station early that morning, and then work on Saturday and Sunday afternoons while his boys were making their way across the country back to Arizona. However, while Jonathan and Joseph were home, Gerald would likewise be at home all of Tuesday and Wednesday.

Among the planned family activities was the entire family trekking together to see the first showing of the day tomorrow, Tuesday, of *Thunder Birds* down at the Senator. That outing was still planned; however, after getting Thomas to finally tell his father the night before what was bothering him, just before he left for work this morning he had told Jonathan and Joseph that he wanted them to go with their younger brother – just the three of them – to see the movie this very afternoon right after Thomas was finished with school. No doubt the older boys would have no problems seeing themselves on the screen in a movie more than once while home on furlough, so the all-family outing for Tuesday still remained. This way, though, the older boys could hopefully help Thomas get over his feelings of becoming distant from his older brothers. Gerald had told them much of what Thomas had spilled to his father, and both Jonathan and Joseph said they would do their best to include Thomas as much as possible this week in what they did.

Gerald's mind was partly on his youngest son this Monday morning; but more than anything, seeing his two oldest sons in their Army Air Forces uniforms brought home to him the reality that his boys would soon be off to war. His mind flashed back to Christmas Eve day last year when Karol Rzepecki came into Gerald's cobbler shop to pick up his shoes before his son Paul's funeral the following week. Paul had been killed during the attack on Pearl Harbor; the first boy from Polish Hill to die in the war. So far at least ten other boys from the neighborhood had been killed, and only God knew how many more would be taken before it was all over. The funerals to date had torn at everyone, and Gerald had to force his mind not to conjure up a horrifying image of the Colemans sitting in Saint Michael's, weeping, with a casket bearing the body of either Jonathan or Joseph directly in front of them...or perhaps an empty casket because there was no body to send to eternal rest.

He forced away those terrible thoughts and tried to concentrate on his work. He was so tired, though. Ever since beginning this job shortly after New Year's Day but still keeping his little cobbler's business going, the brutally long hours, day after day, and the sheer exhaustion that came with that schedule caused Gerald to question almost every single day just what in the world he had gotten himself into. He constantly reminded himself of the reason – doing his part for the war effort by taking a job in this particular plant, even though he was a middle-aged man closing in on forty-five – but the overwhelming fatigue so often dulled his sense of purpose to the point where he frequently questioned his own power of reason for having taken on this commitment. He wouldn't quit – especially not when his sons would soon be doing their best to take the fight to the enemy – but for a man so used to valiantly and stoically working long hours with every fiber of his body, Gerald found himself wondering just what toll this obligation would eventually take on him.

This Monday morning, Gerald did the same thing he did several times each day when the weariness threatened to overcome him. He took a deep breath, said to himself "Enough!" and then grabbed his clipboard as he headed out from his tiny shift supervisor's corner to the rest of the factory floor to do his part for the war effort by helping ensure the highest quality of the shoes and boots for the country's boys and men in uniform.

*   *   *

After the morning's visit to Schenley High, Jonathan and Joseph wandered around the Oakland section of the city. Showing off their Air Corps uniforms hadn't been quite the kick they had expected it to be. The homecoming aspect had certainly been there with about two dozen others home on furlough, as anticipated, also wandering the school's halls. But the renewal of acquaintances had somber overtones since almost every individual conversation eventually came around to some former teammate or other buddy who was now already fighting on one of the fronts. Talking about Jack Leonard who was way over there on Guadalcanal at this very moment, or Reuben Goldfarb on a submarine somewhere in the Atlantic or Pacific – who knew? – or Harry Spitz already flying bombing raids over Europe quickly took any gaiety out of seeing one another. Mostly the conversations ended with proclamations of "take it easy over there" or similar sentiments; there was almost no mention of getting together again, during or after the war, as if even uttering such words might cause a curse to fall on the speaker and the listeners...

Jonathan and Joseph headed in the other direction away from Polish Hill, into the heart of Oakland, and towards the skyscraping University of Pittsburgh's Cathedral of Learning building. No doubt there would be pretty college girls there who would give two men in uniform a second look, a sweet smile, and perhaps even some conversation. And then, who knew...

"You hungry?" Jonathan asked his brother.

"Yeah, a little," Joseph replied. "Ma gave us each a couple huge stacks of hotcakes but I've been thinking about eating something for lunch."

Jonathan looked at his watch. It was only 11:15 in the morning but if they were back at Thunderbird Field they would have just been finishing wolfing down their lunch. Of course, at Thunderbird breakfast was usually at oh-six-hundred hours, right after their 45 minutes of morning calisthenics and their first two-mile run of the day, while this morning they had enjoyed the luxury of sleeping for hours longer than they usually did and had eaten breakfast only a couple hours earlier. Still, both boys were getting hungry.

"Seems strange deciding ourselves when we're going to eat lunch, ya know?" Joseph said.

"Yeah," Jonathan agreed, "and where. Even on the trains across the country we didn't have any choice. Now for a couple whole days we can wander into whatever place we want, at any time, and eat whatever we feel like."

"Well, yeah, except for when Ma tells us when we're eating and what," Joseph corrected his brother who chuckled in response.

"Yeah, that's for sure," Jonathan agreed.

"Anyway," Jonathan continued, "What do you say about Jack Canter's? Roast beef sandwiches?"

Joseph could feel his mouth instantly begin watering.

"Oh man!" he said. "Let's go!"

The Coleman boys headed a few blocks to the corner of Forbes and Atwood, not far from the University, and even though it was still early the place was already beginning to fill up. Upon seeing the two Colemans enter, both in their Army Air Forces uniforms, two Ma Bell workmen each grabbed their remaining sandwich halves and vacated two adjoining stools.

"Here," one of the phone company men said, "You guys take these. We'll finish these on the way back."

"Thanks," both Colemans replied almost in unison. As they sat down and the waitress came to clear the places, the other Ma Bell man looked back and, taking note of their specific uniforms, asked them:

"You guys flyin' yet?"

Jonathan answered with a highly abbreviated version of where the brothers were in their Air Corps training at that point, and mentioned Thunderbird Field as part of his reply.

"Well," the phone company man who had asked the question said, "you guys make sure you after you leave Arizona and head over there you drop a bomb on Hitler or Tojo for me, okay? And stay safe up there." The man pointed skyward as he finished talking.

"We will, thanks," Jonathan replied and the phone company men headed outside.

The brothers each ordered a roast beef sandwich and a cup of coffee. Jonathan reached for a Chesterfield and handed it to his brother, then took one for himself. He flicked open his Zippo, lit Joseph's first then his own.

The sandwiches quickly arrived and Jonathan had just taken his first bite when he looked towards the door of the deli and suddenly stopped chewing when he saw Francine Donner walk inside, accompanied by another pretty young woman who appeared to be about the same age as Francine.

Joseph noticed his brother had suddenly stiffened and followed Jonathan's gaze towards the door. Upon recognizing Francine he groaned and muttered, "Oh, *great*, look who's…"

Jonathan's head spun and he shot an icy look at his brother who immediately stopped talking. Jonathan then looked back towards the door as Francine was scanning the diner looking for a place for her and her friend to sit. When her gaze crossed the counter from left to right she saw Jonathan Coleman staring back at her, and they locked eyes.

* * *

"Is that *him?*" Abby Sobol, Francine's friend who was also a secretary at the War Production Board field office, whispered when she noticed Francine staring at the uniformed young man sitting at the counter.

Francine either didn't hear or simply chose not to answer. Abby was about to ask the question again but realized that she already had her answer.

For a moment, all four remained frozen: Francine and her friend Abby standing by the doorway, Jonathan and

Joseph seated at the counter and looking back at the girls. Finally, Jonathan broke the stalemate by getting up and beginning to walk over to Francine.

Joseph started to reach out to grab his brother's arm but Jonathan was already beyond his brother's reach.

"Oh my God, you look so...so...you know, in your uniform," Francine practically gushed when Jonathan made it to within earshot of the girls and halted.

"Hi Francine," he said. Nothing more, though, as his brain whirled to produce a script for his mouth. Should he say he was glad to see her? Not say anything of the kind? Apologize once again for his bitter words back in February?

"Aren't you going to introduce us?" Abby Sobol interjected just as the silence began to feel awkward.

Francine did indeed make the introductions, careful to introduce him simply as "Jonathan." No "my old boyfriend" or any other amplification, which Jonathan took as this girl Abby already knowing at least part of the story.

Jonathan shook hands briefly with her and as he turned around he noticed that the two seats at the counter to the left of his had just opened up. Two suit-clad businessmen were headed in that direction so he yelled as loudly as he could to his brother:

"Grab those two!"

For a second or two Joseph was tempted to pretend he hadn't heard what his brother or understood the waving hand motion Jonathan had made. He didn't like Francine at all anymore after what she had done with Donnie last year and what the discovery of that indiscretion had done to Jonathan. Especially after sharing six months of Army

Air Forces training, day by day, with his brother, Joseph had no desire to see Jonathan regress to the mess he had been last Christmas Eve and much of Christmas Day. The two brothers had even wound up in a fist-fight at home in the waning moments of Christmas Eve...all because of Francine.

He knew, though, that Jonathan would be furious with him if he ignored the request so he immediately got up and walked over to the two vacated stools as the waitress was swiftly cleaning the places.

"Sorry, the ladies over there are joining us; hope you guys don't mind," he said to the two guys with intentions on those counter seats. Both of the men were at least ten years older than him and Joseph couldn't help but think that if this was a year or more ago – if there weren't a war on, and if Joseph weren't standing there in a military uniform – these two guys would have either ignored him or perhaps shoved him out of the way with a dismissive "beat it, kid!" Now, though, the two men took a quick look at Joseph and then back towards the door where they saw Jonathan leading the two girls in that direction, and they both simply nodded and began searching for somewhere else to sit. No doubt they were in no mood to pick a bone with a kid younger than them who had already joined up while they were walking around in civies, apparently not yet feeling the call of duty to enlist or having gotten caught up in the draft.

The three of them arrived just as Joseph was headed back to his seat. He turned briefly and mustered a touch of pleasantness – just a touch, though – as he said,

"Hey there, Francine. Howya doin'?"

"Hello Joseph," she answered, immediately realizing that Joseph was not particularly thrilled to see her, and probably didn't think very highly of her. She wasn't surprised at all; the few times earlier in the year she had encountered him before he left with Jonathan for Arizona he had done little more than snarl at her as they passed on the street, and the one time she had called out to ask how Jonathan was doing he simply ignored her and kept walking.

Francine broke through the tension by introducing Abby to Joseph and it was funny to notice the smoldering disdain in Joseph's eyes immediately dissolve and give way to that look boys get in that first instant they meet a girl they think they might be interested in.

She looked over at Abby as she was shaking hands with Joseph, and saw the same look in her eyes.

Well, this is an interesting turn of events, Francine thought to herself, before she looked back at the other young man in uniform; the one whom she hadn't seen since that encounter back in February and who, not long before that, had been prepared to ask for Francine's hand before she had made such a mess of things.

*   *   *

Soon after Francine and Abby each ordered The Secretary's Special – a peach half filled with cottage cheese and accompanied by a couple of Melba toast pieces – Jonathan and Joseph began telling the girls about Army Air Forces training at Thunderbird Field out in Arizona. Ordinarily Joseph would have remained mostly quiet given how he felt about Francine, but this girl Abby Sobol...well, he wanted to make sure this girl knew about his solo flying and how he was currently rated third in their class – two places ahead of Jonathan, even – and the suffocating heat out in Arizona during summertime…all of it. Just before the girls' meals were served, Joseph suggested that they shuffle seats a bit. Abby had been sitting left-most at the counter among the four of them so Francine could sit next to Jonathan, with Joseph at the far right.

"How 'bout Francine and I switch so I can tell Abby more about flight training and Arizona while you two catch up?" Joseph offered. A smirk quickly came to Francine's lips and she looked across Jonathan to Joseph, her eyes signaling something along the lines of *"I know what you really have in mind!"* as she reached for her plate and her coffee, nodding in agreement as she did.

The single conversation became two. Joseph remembered what Jonathan had told him once back in August when the cadets had gotten a short off-base pass from Thunderbird one Sunday and the two of them, along with four of their new buddies, had taken a streetcar into Phoenix's sleepy downtown area in hopes of meeting a few Arizona cowgirls.

"Keep asking her about herself," Jonathan had told his brother. "Make sure you don't keep flapping your gums about yourself, okay?"

And so Joseph Coleman told himself to do exactly that as he slid onto the stool Francine had just vacated. He learned that Abby was the same age as he was – eighteen – and had also graduated this past June, though from Peabody High. She lived with her parents, two sisters, and three brothers – a good-sized Slavic Catholic family – in the East Liberty section of the city. Before the war began her parents had intended for her to go to the women's college at Mount Mercy but with all the uncertainty caused by Pearl Harbor and how badly the war news had been throughout much of 1942, they decided that Abigail (as they referred to their daughter) would be better off taking a job as a secretary at the War Production Board field office and waiting at least a little longer before thinking about college.

"And that's where I met Francine," she told Joseph. "Our desks are right next to each other and even though we're so terribly busy all day, we have lots of chances to talk for a little bit at a time."

All the while she spoke Joseph drank in her looks: dark brown hair; about as tall as Francine, maybe five feet, two inches; slender; pretty face, maybe not Gene Tierney or Jean Harlow bombshell gorgeous, but definitely very pretty.

And she smiled a lot; a warm, inviting smile, Joseph thought.

She spooned a small amount of cottage cheese into her mouth and after swallowing continued speaking.

"I went with my parents last week to see a movie about that Air Corps training base you're at," she continued.

"*Thunder Birds*! We're both in that movie!" Joseph said excitedly.

"You're not!"

"We are! Swear! We saw it on base when it came out last month and we're in at least two scenes in the beginning..."

Abby searched her memory, trying to think about what scenes these two might have been in and still wondering if this Joseph Coleman was just pulling her leg, trying to impress her.

"We're going to take our brother Tommy, he's younger than us, to see the movie this afternoon because our Pop wants us to spend some time just with him while we're home. But maybe tomorrow night you want to go see the movie again even though you saw it already, and I'll point out where Jonathan and I are?"

Jonathan had overheard this last bit of conversation. He turned to his left and tapped his brother on the shoulder.

"You forgetting we're going tomorrow for the first show with the whole family?"

Joseph shrugged.

"So I see it even one more time while we're home, ya know? I mean, how often is it that we're in the movies? You know after we get back there we won't have the chance to see it again."

Jonathan also shrugged, then looked back at Francine. So far their own conversation had been superficial; much the same as Joseph's and Abby's without all the "getting to know you" exchanges since, of course, that was unnecessary for these two.

Superficial, but – given everything that had transpired – surprisingly not strained. Maybe time did indeed heal all wounds…or at least some?

"You want to go see it also?"

Francine slowly smiled and lowered her voice until she was fairly certain only Jonathan would be able to hear her, since Joseph had once again resumed talking to Abby.

"Are you asking me out on a date?"

Jonathan was immediately flustered. He started to say "no" then "yes" then "no" again. Truthfully, he didn't exactly know *what* he was asking Francine.

"Yes," she replied when she saw how tongue-tied Jonathan suddenly was. "I'd love to go see you *in* the movies."

Jonathan recovered somewhat even though Francine had laid her left hand on top of his as she answered. Her touch instantly released a flood of long-suppressed memories.

"Okay," he nodded, "but I have to warn you that I have a big love scene with Gene Tierney..."

This time Francine laughed as she withdrew her hand.

"I'll *bet* you do," she said. Then her joviality was instantly replaced by a far-away, mournful look.

"I'm so sorry, Jonathan," she whispered so only he could hear, her eyes beginning to water.

He knew what she meant: Donnie; the engagement that wouldn't be; all of it. He felt his own eyes begin to glisten but refused to look away. He smiled tightly; sadly.

"I know," he whispered back. "I'm sorry too for what I said that one day..."

Francine forced a big smile on her face as she reached for her purse to find sixty cents to pay for her lunch.

"We have to get back," she said. "They only give us forty-five minutes for lunch and we get docked if we get back late. But I can't wait to see your big love scene with Gene Tierney tomorrow night."

Joseph hadn't heard the original exchange and turned around to look at his brother, puzzled.

"Just a joke," Jonathan said when he saw the quizzical look on Joseph's face.

Joseph nodded and then turned back to Abby, who was also fishing for coins to pay for her lunch.

"He *is* just joking," Joseph said to her. "*I'm* the one who has the big love scene with Gene Tierney..."

"In your dreams, flyboy," was Abby Sobol's laughing response.

* * *

Joseph did almost all the talking for the first mile of their walk back home. He tried to play it cool by mixing any number of topics into his near-monologue, but the conversation always seemed to come back to Abby Sobol. Jonathan half-listened to his brother's ramblings and offered a metered series of "uh-huhs" and "yeah" and "yups" along the way, but not much more. Mostly his thoughts were...well, elsewhere.

Finally, just as the boys crossed Centre Avenue and began the trek up Herron Avenue to head home to Polish Hill, Joseph asked Jonathan:

"So whatcha gonna do about Francine?"

Jonathan looked over at his brother but before he could respond, Joseph continued.

"I mean, you gonna take her out to the movie tomorrow night, sweet-talk her, and then love her and leave her?"

Jonathan's eyes widened.

"What?" he demanded.

"You know," Joseph continued. "Get her back for Donnie."

Jonathan felt the rage quickly build but then just as quickly subside. He was furious with his brother for suggesting such a thing…but then hadn't he himself thrown much the same words in Francine's face standing at the streetcar stop that day back in February?

He sighed.

"No," he said quietly – but still through clenched teeth, he wanted Joseph to know that he was out of bounds with that comment and didn't want to hear such a thing again – "I'm not going to love her and leave her, or anything like that. I don't know, I just think that…"

He stopped, not being able to summon the correct words to convey just how he felt…largely because Jonathan simply didn't know *how* he felt at this moment, other than desperately confused.

Joseph looked over at his brother.

"You still in love with her?" he asked.

Jonathan looked back.

"I don't know; maybe; I don't know…" his voice trailed off.

Joseph shrugged and was quiet for a moment, then turned back towards Jonathan.

"How would you feel marrying her knowing that she had…you know, with Donnie."

Jonathan just shook his head and didn't answer as they kept walking. Much of the rest of the walk home was quiet as Jonathan pondered that question that his brother had put to him so bluntly.

*   *   *

Thomas Coleman walked in the front door of the house just as the grandfather clock was chiming to signal that the time was now a quarter to four. He was surprised to see his two brothers sitting in the living room, listening to the Philco. He recognized Judy Garland's voice singing alongside some man's, probably from her new movie. He didn't know the song but given how often the phrase "for me and my gal" was repeated, he figured that might be the title.

Neither Jonathan nor Joseph was wearing his uniform, Thomas immediately noticed. Both were wearing dungarees, long-sleeve work shirts, and white Converses and looked much as they had as long as Thomas could remember before heading away to the Army Air Forces.

"Done for the week now?" Jonathan asked Thomas as the younger boy laid his books on the end table. They wouldn't rest there for long – Ma wouldn't hear of it – but his left arm was tired from lugging the heavy text books and his two loose leaf notebooks all the way home from school.

"Yeah," Thomas said.

"You don't got nothin' goin' on now, right?" Joseph this time.

Thomas shook his head.

"Nah, no homework for the rest of the week. I was just going to wait for Pop to get home for dinner and…"

Jonathan interrupted.

"How 'bout the three of us take a streetcar down to the Senator and watch *Thunder Birds*?"

Thomas was confused.

"I though we were all going together tomorrow when Pop is off work."

"We still are," Joseph chimed in. "But this way the three of us can go together and you can see first-hand what we do most days out there. You know, pal around together just like before we left."

Both of the older brothers could see the instant flush of gratification come to the younger boy's face. Perhaps he had an inkling that this jaunt was contrived rather than spontaneous, but Thomas obviously didn't care.

"Show starts in an hour," Jonathan said. "Let's grab the streetcar in fifteen minutes, okay?"

"Sure," Thomas replied and grabbed his textbooks from the table where had placed them a moment earlier, then headed upstairs to drop them in his room and wash up. While he was upstairs Irene Coleman wandered into the living room with three plates of pumpkin pie remaining from yesterday afternoon's bounty. Jonathan and Joseph had each had a piece of apple pie after returning home an hour or so earlier, but they were certainly not going to say "no" to yet another piece of pie.

"You'll be back for late supper around 7:15?" She asked her eldest as she handed him his plate.

"Sure," Jonathan replied. Arrangements had been made for Gerald, Irene, and the girls to eat supper after Gerald got home from work but the boys would eat separately as soon as they returned from the Senator. Jonathan and Joseph had already prepared their mother and, earlier that morning, their father that after dinner the two of them were going out by themselves for a little while as they had earlier in the day. Both parents agreed that their sons should have a balance between family time and "home on furlough" time until they stepped back on the train in the Friday morning darkness.

Thomas came down the stairs into the living room and took the plate of pumpkin pie from his mother, anxiously gulping the slice down in only four quick bites.

"You ready?" Jonathan asked.

Thomas could only nod since his mouth was stuffed full of pie crust and pumpkin filling as he did his best to chew as quickly as he could.

Joseph walked over to the hall closet and grabbed his and Jonathan's A-2 jackets; the leather flight jackets that the Army's pilots wore when they swaggered here and there. He also grabbed one of his own civilian jackets that he hadn't worn since the earliest days of this past spring. He took his own A-2 and tossed it to Thomas.

"Here," he said to Thomas as he also handed Jonathan's flight jacket to his older brother at the same time, "You wear this, I'll wear my other jacket."

Thomas started to protest but Joseph continued.

"I want to wear a civie jacket just to remember what it feels like not to wear a uniform, you know? Besides this way you can look aces."

Thomas was only an inch and a half shorter than Joseph and had about the same build, so the A-2 fit him perfectly when he eagerly put it on.

"Thanks," he said gratefully. For at least the next couple hours, perhaps the old Coleman boys triumvirate would be on display, he thought.

Thomas did indeed catch a few glances from the other passengers on the streetcar ride down Liberty Avenue. His youngish face betrayed his age and it was doubtful anyone thought that he himself was an Army Air Forces flyer, but most people probably pieced together that this boy was traveling with the other young man wearing an A-2 as well as the third one wearing the civie jacket but who looked like he might be the brother of the other two.

Tickets at the Senator were fifty cents each (tomorrow's would be only thirty cents because of the before-3:00 matinee pricing) and the boys settled into their seats just in time to stand again for The Star Spangled Banner. After plopping themselves in their seats once more the *Movietone News* appeared with, of course, the latest war news from North Africa, Guadalcanal, and the fierce battle between the Russians and the Nazis. Then they settled in for the MGM cartoon: *Blitz Wolf*, a takeoff on the Three Little Pigs story with Hitler as the wolf.

And then it was time for *Thunder Birds*. Joseph leaned to his left and whispered to Thomas, who was sitting between his older brothers,

"We're coming up a couple minutes after the Air Corps song. I'll poke you."

Thomas nodded eagerly, anxiously awaiting his brothers' appearance on the very screen in front of his eyes while he listened to the soaring refrains of "Off we go, into the wild blue yonder…"

Then the narrator's voice, dramatically beginning with "This is Thunderbird the field…" Some close-ups of some of the actual Chinese and British flying cadets who trained alongside the Army's pilots. The narrator then smoothly transitioning to "And here are American boys…" just as the face of a young actor portraying a pilot filled the screen.

Then, a moment later, a squadron of American flying cadets came marching up and Joseph recognized himself in the second row. This appearance wasn't one the Coleman boys had previously caught when they saw the movie the first time.

"There I am! Second row!" Joseph said, his voice louder than he intended, and several people in the theater turned around to see who had spoken those words.

Thomas' eyes – Jonathan's as well – immediately looked towards the second row and sure enough, there was Corporal Joseph Coleman, marching in his A-2 jacket and wearing his leather flying cap and goggles propped up on his forehead. Jonathan's eyes searched the group for his own image but the scene shifted before he could find himself.

Then, less than a minute later, there they were both were in a classroom shot, sitting side by side. This scene they had taken note of and were ready for its appearances. Joseph nudged Thomas again, who immediately caught the sight of his brothers.

They had apparently been cut from the very short baseball and basketball scenes as they had suspected after seeing the movie the first time. They had been there that day and had certainly been filmed. But when they saw the movie back in Phoenix they couldn't find themselves, and sure enough this time around they were absent from those scenes. But they did find themselves one more time, running in formation in their gray sweatshirts and sweatpants.

They all agreed the movie was corny, with ridiculous dialogue such as Gene Tierney telling her former lover

Preston Foster during their first encounter early in the movie that the reason they hadn't worked out when they had known each other before was because she "came off the line a woman...not a P-38." Still, both Jonathan and Joseph could tell as they snuck glances at their younger brother throughout the movie that Thomas was in heaven, sitting in the chilly Senator theater wearing Joseph's A-2 jacket and watching a movie about the place where his brothers were going through training...with his brothers having made several cameo appearances on the screen right before his eyes!

The movie finally concluded, the boys filed out of the theater and headed back to the streetcar stop for the ride back home for dinner. Thomas was especially animated the entire way home, asking about the flying scenes from the movie and if that's what things at Thunderbird Field were really like. Jonathan and Joseph took turns filling in the blanks in the tale told by the movie, telling stories of aerial maneuvers in the PT-17 Army trainer (and maneuvering their hands to indicate flying formations the way most flyboys did), and before they knew it they were walking up the front steps to their house.

All through dinner Thomas couldn't stop relating in great detail what they had just seen until finally Gerald looked over at his son and said, "Tommy, don't spoil the movie for us; we're all going to see it tomorrow, right?"

Thomas Coleman just grinned and said, "That's right, Pop; and I can't wait."

* * *

After dinner and dessert Jonathan and Joseph, as agreed, headed back out for an evening of...well, they weren't quite certain. The idea was to make the rounds of a bar or two back in Oakland and see who else they might run into. Originally, their intention had been not so much to look for old friends – that had already occurred earlier in the day when they stopped by Schenley High – but to see what girls they might be able to impress and get to know better. Now, though, after Jonathan's lunchtime encounter with Francine Donner and Joseph having met Abby Sobol, meeting new girls was off the evening's agenda. (Or, as Joseph put it when they were waiting for the streetcar to take them to Oakland, "I'm taking meeting a couple of dames off of the pre-flight checklist, okay?") Still, they did change back into their Army Air Forces uniforms and put on their flight jackets to cut the crisp fall chill.

"Hey, isn't that Joey DeMarco over there at the end?" Joseph nodded towards the far end of the bar at Dominic's Tavern, the Oakland bar they had selected as their first stop since it was only a few steps from the streetcar stop where they jumped off.

Jonathan looked in the direction that his brother had indicated and recognized the face. Dominic's was filled with young men wearing one kind of uniform or another and Joey DeMarco was no exception. Jonathan and Joseph both knew that DeMarco had gone into the Army and had headed off to basic training at Keesler Field the same day that both Colemans had boarded the first of the trains to take them to Phoenix and Thunderbird Field.

Both of the Josephs – Joseph DeMarco, who almost always was known as Joey, and Joseph Coleman, more often than not referred to by his proper name because that's how his mother wanted it – had been in the most recent Schenley High School graduating class back in June.

Both had played on the Schenley football team but whereas Joseph Coleman was mostly a second- and third-stringer who saw little playing time, Joey DeMarco had been one of the stars their senior year…essentially Jonathan Coleman's successor as one of the team leaders. In fact, even though both of the Josephs had been in the same class, Joey DeMarco was actually somewhat closer friends with Jonathan by virtue of their respective football abilities. Still, Joey DeMarco and Joseph Coleman were good enough pals. Joey DeMarco hadn't been among the Schenley alums who had been at the school earlier today, at least while the Colemans had been there.

Jonathan and Joseph wove their way through the crowd at Dominic's, scanning the faces they walked by to see if anyone else looked familiar. Nobody so far, and it was just as they approached that Joey DeMarco happened to turn around and see the brothers.

A big smile came to his face.

"Coleman!" he said, referring mostly to Jonathan but since he also called Joseph the same, especially after Jonathan had graduated, his greeting was sort of a two-in-one effort.

"DeMarco!" Jonathan said as he extended his hand.

After shaking hands with Jonathan, Joey DeMarco then did likewise with Joseph.

"How's the flyboy business?" he said to both of them. "You guys are out in Arizona, right?"

"Uh-huh," Joseph answered.

"So far so good," Jonathan added. "We're all done with Pre-Flight and about three-fourths of the way through Primary in the PT-17, and in a couple weeks we move on to Basic." Jonathan, like his brother, had easily adopted the shorthandish military lingo when referring to the various stages of their training.

"Not sure where we're going after Thunderbird for Advanced," Joseph chimed in. "Maybe they'll keep us in Phoenix and send us to Williams Field and then Luke, you know?"

"So how about you?" Jonathan asked. "How long you home on furlough for?"

A smile came to Joseph DeMarco's face.

"Believe it or not, this ain't furlough; the Army, in their infinite wisdom, stationed me in Pittsburgh."

Both of the Colemans looked at each other and then back at their high school buddy.

"You pulling my leg?" Jonathan asked.

"Nah," Joseph DeMarco said, looking at his empty glass of Duquesne.

"I was getting ready to get outta here and go home to the missus," he said, "But I'll stay and have another one."

The grin came back to his face.

"I love telling people about being stationed here, they always react just about the same as you did."

He looked back towards the bar, caught the bartender's eye, and held up three fingers after pointing to his empty glass.

"I'm buying, guys," DeMarco said. Jonathan started to protest but Joey cut him off.

"How about we say this: you guys will both be officers and I'm always gonna be an enlisted man, so how about after the war we get together here and you guys buy me a beer, okay?"

The reference to "after the war" wasn't lost on any of them – even Joey DeMarco, for now apparently stationed right here in good old Pittsburgh, Pennsylvania – but none of the three wanted to add any sort of "okay, if…" caveat to Joey's declaration. Jonathan and his brother just nodded and the moment the bartender brought the three Duquesnes the two bar stools to the left of Joey DeMarco vacated; the Colemans quickly sat down.

"So here's to the good old Schenley football team," Joey DeMarco said, raising his glass. Three glasses came together before each of them took a healthy swig.

"So what's this about getting stationed here?" Jonathan added.

"Well," Joey began, "you remember I married Roseanne right after graduation, right?"

The two Colemans nodded. Roseanne Conte had been a classmate of both Joey DeMarco and Joseph Coleman, and she had begun dating Joey last October near the beginning of their senior year, right after the homecoming game. Joey had popped the question back in April when he decided to enlist in the Army and the two of them were married in early June, a few days before Joey boarded the train to Biloxi and basic training.

"Well," he continued, "I'm getting close to the end of training, wondering if they're going to ship me off to England or Africa or maybe out to the Pacific when here comes my orders. I look and they say '76th Air Defense Battery, Pittsburgh, Pennsylvania.' I figure someone is playing a joke on me, ya know? So I start looking for the joker cause I don't think this is real funny and I go to find out that it's totally legit. The Army decides to assign me to the air defense guns they're putting in around a bunch of the steel mills in case the Krauts try to bomb us."

"For how long?" Joseph Coleman asked. "I mean, is that for a year and then they'll send you somewhere else?"

Joey DeMarco shrugged as he took another swig from his glass and realized that he had finished yet another. Without missing a beat he nodded again to the bartender who laid down three more refills, even though Joseph and Jonathan were only half-done with theirs, and took Joey's quarter while plunking down a dime in the same smooth motion.

"I got these," Joey said when he saw both Joseph and Jonathan reaching for their pockets. His words were starting to slur a bit though, and both of the Colemans wondered just how long their high school buddy had been sitting here in Dominic's slugging down Duquesnes.

"Anyways," Joey continued, "I dunno how long. It could be six months or a year, or for all I know it could be as long as the whole damn war lasts. Wouldn't that be a hoot? I spend the entire war living in my Pop's house while you guys and everyone else are out there doin' the fightin', ya know?"

"Hey, let me tell you," Jonathan said as he finished his first beer and reached for the second Duquesne Joey had bought. "If that's the way it plays out then so be it. Besides, you never know when the Luftwaffe might try to bomb New York or Washington or come up here and try to take out the steel mills. That's what we're doing to theirs right now and you know we're going to start heading farther and farther into Germany as the war goes on. So I think they'll try the same thing here eventually, so you manning an anti-aircraft gun is every bit as much fighting the war as us flying into theirs. At least that's the way I see it."

"I s'pose," Joey slurred. But both of the Coleman boys were feeling increasingly unsettled by where this conversation was going. The truth was that both thought it very unlikely that the Nazis would ever be able to muster a bombing attack against any of the steel mills in or around Pittsburgh. Last year, in the immediate aftermath of Pearl Harbor, such fears had seemed very real. Now, though, after taking the fight to the enemy in North Africa and over in the Pacific, worries about attacks along the coasts and especially inland had significantly diminished. That probably meant that sometime down the road Joey DeMarco would get uprooted from his cushy assignment, where he was living for the time being in his boyhood home *and sleeping with his wife, for heaven's sakes,* and get sent to some far-off battlefield.

But these things were best left unspoken.

"So how's Roseanne?" Joseph asked. He had had his eye on Roseanne Conte back in their sophomore year but instead she had started going out with Tony Cortese, the guy she had dated for a while until dumping Tony for Joey DeMarco.

"She's good," Joey's mood brightened a bit. "She was a little bit strange when I came home from Keesler Field and didn't seem to really believe that I was getting stationed at home. But she's good, ya know?"

"Hey," Joey said, remembering something all of a sudden as he looked over at Jonathan. "What's up with you and Francine? You getting back together with her while you're home? I never did figure out why you two broke up…"

His voice trailed off. Jonathan had long realized that he didn't know, and might never know, how many of his Schenley High buddies knew about what had happened between Francine and Donnie Yablonski. Lord knows Jonathan hadn't told anybody, and he was fairly certain that

Francine hadn't spilled her shameful secret to any of her own girlfriends. After all, what kind of girl would tell her friends about getting so drunk that she had gone all the way with a different guy than the one everyone knew was getting ready to ask for her hand in marriage?

That left Donnie Yablonski. There were times that Jonathan was certain that Donnie had slunk away out of Pittsburgh right after Christmas without saying a word to anyone about what he had done with – to – Francine, but other times Jonathan couldn't help but feel that Donnie had bragged about his conquest to at least a few of his closest friends, and they in turn would spread the word. However, during the almost seven months between that night and when Jonathan left for Thunderbird Field, he hadn't heard a snicker or whisper that led him to believe Donnie had indeed smeared Francine's name. Very likely he had bragged to some of his new sailor buddies up at the big naval training base in Chicago about what he had done shortly before leaving Pittsburgh, and it was always possible that others from Pittsburgh who were going through training there would pick up the story.

It didn't matter, Jonathan thought to himself as these thoughts passed through his head, lightning-fast, as Joey DeMarco asked him about getting back together with Francine. This guy obviously didn't know; as drunk as he apparently was, Joey certainly would have slurred something about Francine's transgression.

"I don't think so," Jonathan replied to the question about getting back together with Francine. "We're just not...you know..."

Joseph came to the rescue and changed the subject.

"So come next baseball season you can go to Forbes Field and see the Pirates play, huh? I guess that's one bonus of being stationed here."

"Yeah, I guess so," Joey replied. "But you know what?"

"Huh?" Joseph replied.

"You never know, you guys might get to fly with someone famous like Hank Greenberg or Jimmy Stewart. Wouldn't that be a kick?"

*   *   *

"You want to walk it?" Jonathan asked his brother as they left Dominic's after each had poured down three beers; there would only be one stop tonight it turned out. Just after 10:00 the temperature was still hovering right around forty degrees and the threat of rain from earlier today seemed to have disappeared for good. Both Jonathan and Joseph felt the need for a half hour's walk to clear their head after the smoky stuffiness at Dominic's, even though they had made this very same trek earlier in the day.

"So what do you make of Joey getting hitched all of a sudden right before he heads off to Keesler Field?" Joseph asked his brother.

Jonathan shrugged, at first wondering about his brother's question. They both had known those two had gotten hitched right after graduation, the same as a couple of other Schenley guys; that was old news.

"I dunno," was his reply as he contemplated the question.

"Do you mean getting married even though he thought he was headed off to the war for maybe a couple of years?"

Jonathan continued. "I mean it worked out for him, winding up right back here after only a couple months at basic. But yeah, suppose he was like nearly every other guy headed off to England or the Pacific, or even some training base in the States. I know lots of guys do that, get married before they ship out, but I don't know how I'd feel having a wife waiting for me back here and not knowing if I'd be coming back in one year or two years, or…you know."

Joseph nodded.

"Yeah, that's what I'm thinking. If it was me I'da probably gotten engaged to Roseanne before I left but held off getting married until I came home."

He had a thought then.

"But suppose while I was away she meets someone else and breaks off the engagement, ya know?"

"Same thing could happen if you're married," Jonathan retorted. "That's what happened to Wilson, and he wasn't gone from home more than four months." Jonathan was referring to one of their Thunderbird classmates, Louis Wilson, who only two weeks earlier had received the shocking news in a letter from his wife of less than five months back up in Montana saying that she had met someone else and wanted a divorce.

"Maybe the best thing is to just forget about any of that until it's all over," Joseph said morosely.

Jonathan looked at his brother as they started up Herron Street for the second time this very day.

"So why you getting all talkative about leaving girls behind all of a sudden?"

Joseph didn't answer right away.

"You just met her," Jonathan continued, knowing exactly what his brother was thinking. "You haven't even gone out on a date with her yet. You talked with her for, what, twenty minutes over lunch?"

"Yeah, I know," Joseph said, a touch irritably. "Just thinking, okay?"

"Yeah, okay," Jonathan answered. He wasn't going to force the issue with his brother's apparent infatuation with Abby Sobol; he had a far more serious predicament of his own in mind as the boys walked the rest of the way home mostly in silence this Monday evening.

3 – Tuesday, November 24, 1942

Jonathan Coleman – Captain Jonathan Coleman in the dream, apparently he had survived enough missions over Germany as a second and first lieutenant to be promoted – was supposed to be paying attention to the gauges in front of him; his navigator's course corrections; the Nazi flak bursting outside the B-17 he was piloting; the Messerschmitt pursuit planes attacking his Flying Fortress; *everything* that was going on around him on this bombing run. Instead, he was again reading the terrible letter that had just been delivered mid-flight by a mailman to the plane's cockpit (in the dream this had seemed perfectly normal):

> *Dear Jonathan,*
>
> *I know it's terrible of me to write you when you are away at war to tell you that I have met another man and need to end our engagement, but that is what I must do. His name is Ronald and he works here in Oakland…*

The letter had gone on in excruciating detail about Francine's first date with Ronald, how nicely he had kissed her, and how she had let this Ronald go all the way with her because she was too drunk…

Jonathan forced himself awake, gasping for the air in his room as if by forcing the atmosphere from the still-darkened bedroom into his lungs he would be immune from falling back into that strange, terrible dream.

He sat up in bed and picked up the alarm clock. Despite the room's darkness and his unfocused vision, the radium-coated numbers and clock hands indicated that it was barely 6:00. Jonathan briefly contemplated trying to fall asleep again after sufficient time had passed to hopefully prevent this latest dream or some variant from recurring, but decided that he might as well get up.

He sat there for a few moments and snatches of scenes from at least two other dreams that night came to him. In one of them he had been standing with Francine at Saint Michael's, Father Nolan about to pronounce them man and wife, when he looked over and saw that Donnie Yablonski was his best man. Even in the dream he felt the rush of revulsion at not only Donnie's presence but Francine's as well, given what had happened. But that was all he recalled from that particular dream, and wasn't sure if Father Nolan had ever completed his pronouncement.

In another dream – this one more realistic than either of the others – he was sitting with Joseph in the ready room of some air base over in England, waiting for the Colonel to enter and brief the men on the day's mission. While they were waiting another pilot sitting behind the two Colemans tapped Jonathan on the shoulder. Jonathan turned around and the first lieutenant proceeded to say that he was from Pittsburgh; that he had gone to Schenley High as well; and that right before he left for England Donnie Yablonski had come back to Pittsburgh and was making time with Francine and she was telling everyone that she was thinking about breaking off her engagement to Jonathan. In the dream, Joseph sadly looked over at

Jonathan when this stranger's tale had concluded and said, simply, "I told you."

Jonathan knew exactly why at least three dreams involving Francine and not-so-happily-ever-after times had happened that night. Truth be told, he was incredibly nervous about going to see *Thunder Birds* with her this very evening. Making that suggestion – following Joseph's lead with Abby Sobol and "sort of" asking Francine on a date – yesterday had been one thing; an impulsive act that seemed the perfect thing to say at that moment. But now, after reflecting for many hours (and apparently during at least three dreams) on tonight's encounter, he wasn't so certain. Sitting there at the Jack Canter's counter, enveloped in Francine's very presence and with sweet memories of times past finally allowed to surface once again; all had seemed right with the world. Now, though, dark memories of hearing Francine utter those terrible words were fighting with those other remembrances for the upper hand.

Oh well, Jonathan thought; sitting here in the darkened bedroom certainly wasn't going to help matters. He stood, walked out into the hallway and then into the bathroom, and after finishing his morning business and brushing his teeth he headed quietly down the stairs, not wanting to wake anyone at this early hour. Chances are his Ma would be awake – she almost always was before 6:00 – but there was no way in the world Charlene, Thomas, or Ruthie would be on this first day of their extended school vacation. Joseph no doubt would be snoring away, and he expected his Pop to likewise still be asleep given his out-of-the-ordinary day off of work and how tired he seemed. For a flash Jonathan allowed a touch of worry for his father's health to enter his consciousness but he forced it away; he could only deal with so much at one time.

Jonathan was correct about his mother being awake, but wrong about his father still being asleep in bed. His parents were sitting together at the kitchen table, each nursing a cup of coffee. They both looked in unison as their oldest child entered the kitchen.

"What are you doing up so early?" Irene asked, the concern immediately apparent in her voice. "Are you feeling all right?"

"I'm fine, Ma; just couldn't sleep any more, that's all."

Satisfied that her son wasn't feeling sick but also knowing that something was on his mind, Irene let the matter drop. She went to the stove and filled a coffee cup for Jonathan.

"Here," she said as she handed the cup to him as Jonathan sat down at the breakfast table. "I'm going to go upstairs to make your bed and clean your room."

"You don't have to do that, Ma," Jonathan protested. "I make my bed good and tight every day out at Thunderbird. I'll do it here."

Jonathan grinned as a thought came to him.

"In fact you'll be able to actually bounce a quarter off of it, just like they show in the movies."

Irene would hear none of it.

"You can go back to making your bed when you get back there," she said. "While you're home you relax." She walked out of the kitchen and both Gerald and Jonathan could hear her quietly take the first few stairs until that sound faded as Irene tried not to wake anybody else.

"She just probably wanted to give us time to talk alone," Jonathan said, looking across the table at his father. Jonathan reached for the morning *Post-Gazette* that was already on the table and took in the headline that told of the Allies taking control of the port of Dakar in French West Africa. Jonathan quickly scanned the news report which also told of the continued political intrigue involving the French Admiral Darlan switching sides from the Vichy French to the Allies and all the repercussions on both the Allied and Axis sides of the war.

Then his eyes were drawn to a photograph of an Army nurse from Ligonier who, according to the caption, had been killed in action in North Africa this past November 14th. Jonathan felt an immediate wash of sorrow; it was sad enough when local boys gave the ultimate sacrifice and had notices of their deaths show up in the newspaper; but a pretty girl like this? She looked like she was only twenty-one or twenty-two, Jonathan figured. My God, this war was terrible, he thought; and it's only just really now getting underway!

Saddened at what he had just seen and read, he laid the paper down without wanting to look at any more, or think about war news, at least for now.

His father came to the rescue.

"How is Joseph doing out there?" he asked quietly; a probing question.

"Good," Jonathan replied. "Really good. He's third in our class right now and is even two places ahead of me."

Gerald nodded.

"I know," he replied, "you boys mentioned that during Sunday dinner. But is he really doing well? Is he thinking clearly when he's flying?"

For a moment Jonathan wasn't quite sure what his father was asking.

"Do you mean is he shooting his mouth off out there about wanting to go shoot down Messerschmitts and become an ace and go on War Bond tours because he's famous; that sort of thing?"

Gerald nodded and Jonathan shook his head in response as he took a sip of the still-piping hot coffee.

"Nah," he said. "He's got a pretty good head on his shoulders now. I know last Christmas after Pearl Harbor he and Marty were running around talking about killing Nazis and Japs and all that, but he stopped most of that a month or two before we left, remember?"

Gerald nodded again.

"Anyway, from the time we got there and especially after they started putting us in the PT-17 for lessons, he got all serious. He's really grown up out there, you know? He's not showing off up in the air, and when he's flying in formation he does great."

"That's good to hear," Gerald answered, sighing with apparent relief. He had been worried about his middle son – both of them actually, but Joseph more than Jonathan – the entire time the boys had been away in Arizona. He certainly read all of their letters, front and back and top to bottom; each one several times. From what the boys had written home things seemed to be going alright for both of them but you could never tell until you heard it with your own ears. And Gerald knew that Jonathan was not one to hide any concerns for his brother's well-being if indeed he had had any; he certainly would have confided in his father if he had been the least bit worried about his brother out there.

"And how about you? You doing okay?" Gerald asked.

"Sure," Jonathan answered. "There's guys there who are better flyers than me, I guess including Joseph, but I'm doing good. No trouble with the academics, and haven't done anything stupid or really wrong up in the air."

He thought about adding "...at least so far" but before the words could leave his mouth Jonathan realized that his father might read the most negative, worry-filled connotation into that phrase and begin to worry even more about Jonathan's well-being; and Joseph's as well. So he just let his statement hang there.

"How are you feeling about what comes after being done with training?"

Jonathan realized that his father was in a particularly probing and communicative mood; something very unlike his normal demeanor. He proceeded to tell Gerald as best as he could what he thought about learning to fly pursuit planes or bombers or transports or whatever type of plane they assigned him to after he was done with training at Thunderbird. He tried to explain how he felt, at least at this point, about what he was expecting when he eventually flew combat missions.

Mostly he tried to satisfy his father's apparent need to learn as much as possible about what his sons would soon be facing. Jonathan Coleman realized that his father's frame of reference about this war came mostly from the newspaper headlines that as much as possible screamed in large bold type about FANTASTIC TURNING-POINT ADVANCES AND VICTORIES or tried to downplay negative news; or in some cases even make "no news" seem as if it were the most thrilling occurrence ever. Last Thursday's *Post-Gazette* that was still sitting in the living room's newspaper rack was a perfect example. The oversized headline had read "ALLIES REPULSE NAZI

PATROLS." Was a minor skirmish in the midst of a major invasion really worthy of such a headline...in extra-large bold capital letters?

Or this morning's paper: underneath the screaming headline about the Allies taking Dakar there was also a two-line smaller headline. The first one read "Russian Offensive Gaining Speed" but the second line noted that "Nazi Planes Slow Allies in Tunisia." Besides the fact that the battles in Russia and North Africa were two very different fronts in the war and really made no sense to include together, the second line about the Nazi planes having some effect against our side certainly wasn't "good news from the war front." Yet it flowed at the top of Page 1 immediately from the more positive headlines almost as if it were, no doubt for reasons of keeping up the morale of those on the Home Front.

Gerald seemed satisfied with what Jonathan told him and got up from the table to refill his coffee. He sat back down with a sigh.

Jonathan hesitated for a moment.

"Pop, can I talk to you about something else?"

"Sure," Gerald said.

Jonathan took in and then blew out a deep breath.

"You know how we're all going to see *Thunder Birds* today?"

Gerald nodded.

"Well," Jonathan continued, "yesterday Joseph and I had lunch in Oakland and Joseph met this girl, and he's taking her tonight to go see the movie even though we saw it last night with Tommy and the whole family is also going to see it again today."

"So Joseph doesn't want to go today?" Gerald asked after doing his best to absorb the meaning of Jonathan's single meandering sentence.

Jonathan shook his head.

"No, nothing like that." He allowed himself a small smile. "We both could see that movie three times each day while we're home, you know?"

He paused before continuing.

"It's that when Joseph and this girl Abby go see the movie tonight, I'm also going along with this other girl."

Gerald looked Jonathan directly in the eyes.

"With Francine?"

Jonathan raised his eyes in response to his father's words.

"How did you know that?" he asked.

"By the way you were talking," his father replied. "If this was some girl you just met like Joseph did, then you would just say that you were going tonight to see the movie again, or maybe not say anything at all."

Jonathan shrugged.

"Yeah, I guess," he said. He hesitated, then asked,

"So what do you think? I mean, after...you know..."

Gerald shrugged and blew out a breath.

"Let me ask you this. How do *you* feel about going to the movies with her? Is this just going to the movies for old time's sakes while you're home, or do you have something else in mind?"

Jonathan shrugged.

"I honestly don't know, Pop." He looked around the kitchen for a moment, then got up again to pour more coffee for himself. This time he didn't sit down again. Instead he came back over to his chair and leaned on it from behind; a pensive posture.

"Yesterday, when I first saw her come into the door at Jack Canter's I didn't really know what to think about her, and wasn't sure if I actually wanted to talk to her. The last time I saw her way back in February I said some pretty bad things to her because I was still so angry, so I figured she wouldn't really want to talk to me anyway. But we started talking at the counter while Joseph was making time with this new girl who's a friend of Francine's, and I honestly forgot all about…you know, what happened."

"So are you thinking about giving it another try with her?"

"Well," Jonathan answered after about fifteen seconds of thought, "it's not like I'm here at home and we could start dating or anything like that to see how things go. And besides…"

He struggled for the right words.

"I just don't know if I could…well, after Donny, I'm not sure how things would really be between us."

Gerald leaned forward, putting his elbows on the kitchen table and clasping his hands into a fist on which he rested his chin. He looked directly at Jonathan.

"Have you been" – Gerald cleared his throat because of the uncomfortable nature of what he was asking his own son – "with any girls since you broke up with her?"

Jonathan hesitated before answering.

"A couple," he said sheepishly. "There was one girl here back in May before I left, and then we had a pass out in Phoenix one Saturday night and I went with a couple of the guys to…"

Jonathan suddenly realized that he shouldn't have started the second part of his sentence, and wondered how his moralistic father would react to this sudden blurting out of his having visited a "house" late on a stifling hot August night in one of the seedier parts of Phoenix…his meaning clear even though Jonathan didn't finish the sentence.

Gerald just nodded.

"How do you think Francine would feel if she knew you had been with those other girls?"

"That's different," Jonathan started to protest. "I wasn't still going with Francine, but when she and Donny…she was almost engaged to me. And besides, I'm a man and she's a woman, so it's different."

Gerald chuckled as he sat back.

"I suppose," he said. "But maybe not all that different."

He sighed. He then looked around to ensure that he and his oldest son were still alone in the kitchen; that his wife was not within earshot.

"Back when I went over to France there were three of us who all joined up together, and the other two fellows had girls. I knew your Ma already but hadn't started courting her yet until I came back and we didn't get engaged until Christmas of '19. You know all that, right?"

Jonathan nodded.

"Well, the other two fellas both were engaged   and one of them had something happen much like with you and Francine, except it was while we were at basic training over at Camp Grant, out in Illinois."

Gerald pronounced the state "Ill-a-noise" as he always had.

"So we get back to Pittsburgh for an entire month before they sent us to New York to ship out for France, and while we were home this fella finds out that his girl had been with this other man, so he breaks off the engagement. We ship out and come back in early '19 after Armistice Day and then we all go to work."

Gerald paused, contemplated yet another cup of coffee, but decided to continue without refilling his cup.

"I ran into him about three years later in a speakeasy and we sat down for a couple of beers and he just about starts crying that he had made a terrible mistake, that he should have just forgiven that girl and married her anyway. He had gotten married to this other girl he met right after coming back from the war and she was a miserable woman. He kept saying that if he had it to do over again, he would have just forgotten all about what that first girl had done and married her."

"Yeah," Jonathan retorted, "but did that first girl still want to marry him until he found out?"

"I guess so," Gerald replied. "She never broke off the engagement while we were at Camp Grant and I think it was just that one time, or maybe a couple; I don't really know for sure. I knew her a little; she was a nice girl, a little mixed up because her Ma had died when she was just a baby and her father didn't really know anything about raising girls. But you leave that thing with the other fella out of it and I could have seen her making a good wife for my friend and mother for his children."

Now Gerald did get up to refill his coffee with the last of what was left in the pot. After sitting back down, he continued.

"Here's what I'm saying. I think that once the war got started for us here, and even before that over in England for them, people started doing things they wouldn't ordinarily do. Fellas will be away at war and their girls or even their wives might, you know, play around. And the soldiers will find girls over there, even if they're married. I'm not saying it's right; I'm just saying that it's going to happen far more than during normal times. And I think because of the war, and all the worry every day, many people will decide to forgive that other person if..."

Jonathan interrupted.

"So are you telling me I *should* get back with Francine?"

Gerald shook his head.

"No, but I'm not telling you not to. I don't know what you should do, and right now you don't know either. I *will* tell you that if you do decide to give it another try with her that you better not go run off and get married tomorrow or the next day before you get back on that train. Maybe you get engaged like you were going to; or maybe you leave things so that when you get back, if you both want to, *then* you'll get engaged and maybe married real quick. For all you know, you might go out with her tonight and realize that you don't really want to be with her at all anymore. But only you can decide that, and something tells me that you'll make up your mind pretty quick and will do the best thing."

With that last line, Gerald reached across with his large workman's hands and laid them both on top of his son's that were folded and resting on the kitchen table. Jonathan had been looking down at his folded hands and upon seeing his father's hands settle on top of his own, he looked up at Gerald. No more words were spoken but the boy's eyes conveyed the gratitude for his father having spoken so openly about matters so personal and private...and uncomfortable.

Jonathan had one last question.

"What about Ma? I mean, how do you think she would feel knowing that Francine had, um..."

Gerald withdrew his hands and reached again for his coffee cup.

"Don't worry about that. If you decide that after all that has happened Francine is the one for you, then I'll talk to your Ma. Okay?"

Jonathan nodded.

"Okay," he replied.

*   *   *

Charlene Coleman spent the better part of the morning in her bedroom, sitting on her bed and staring at the calling card bearing Gene Kelly's printed name and hand-scribbled telephone number out in Hollywood...and daydreaming. Rehearsals for the All-City High School War Bond Benefit would resume this afternoon, and for the first time since that magical encounter with Gene Kelly she would be up on stage singing with Sammy Canter and then by herself. No doubt she would be looking across at Sammy during their number and instead seeing the dapper Broadway dancer who had taken notice of her. And during her solo performance of *Bewitched, Bothered, and Bewildered* she would be fearlessly singing on a stage in front of a conjured Broadway audience rather than the empty seats.

How glorious it all was! She scooted her knees towards her chin and leaned forward, smiling sweetly, wrapping her arms around her legs just below her knees in that classic pose of a daydreaming teenage girl. For a split second she imagined flashbulbs were going off around her in her room as notebook-bearing reporters took turns asking Charlene about her new movie in which MGM had just assigned her the starring role. Clark Gable was to be her co-star, and a few moments earlier he had given his own interview to the movie reporters saying that working with Miss Charlene Coleman would be an even bigger treat for him than with Vivian Leigh. The poor man was still mourning the loss of his beloved Carole Lombard, but there had been that Rhett Butler twinkle in his eye when he was first introduced to Miss Charlene Coleman, so perhaps while filming this new epic...

Charlene's daydreaming about Clark Gable was interrupted by a sudden troubling thought. Would she have to change her name as so many other actresses did? She pondered the question for a while as she thought of glamorous stage names and decided that as long as she could remain "Charlene" the studio could change her last name to *anything* else they wanted it to be. After all, she had spent the better part of late last year and the beginning of this year thinking of herself as Mrs. Charlene Moncheck after Larry's "proposal" shortly before last Christmas. She giggled at the silly thought of seeing *that* name – Charlene Moncheck – up there on the marquee outside the Strand next to the name of Clark Gable or Gary Cooper...or Gene Kelly.

The daydreams continued throughout the morning for Charlene, and by the time she heard her mother's voice mustering the Coleman children together to get ready to go see their brothers in *Thunder Birds*, Charlene felt that yes indeed, all was right with the world...or at least her little corner of it.

*　　*　　*

The streetcar ride down to the Senator reprised the one the boys had taken the previous afternoon with Thomas wearing an A-2 flight jacket – Jonathan's this time, though – and drawing occasional stares from the other passengers. The morning's cold drizzle had stopped and the temperature was hovering right around forty degrees, where it was expected to remain and in fact even go up a few degrees throughout the day and this evening. Irene Coleman naturally made sure that everyone in her family – Gerald included – was tightly bundled up against the elements even though by the time they all hopped off the trolley each one of them was beginning to perspire from wearing a scarf and gloves at Irene's insistence.

Once inside the theater they all shed their winter outerwear and grabbed seven choice seats. Irene sat on the left of the family and Gerald all the way to the right, with Ruthie between her mother and Charlene. Joseph sat in the middle of them all with Thomas seated between his father and Jonathan. Over Irene's protest that lunch would be spoiled, all of her children were already gorging on popcorn, pop, and Hershey bars procured from the concession stand. Gerald had convinced her that this was a very special occasion, not just "any old outing" at the movies, so copious amounts of candy and popcorn and quarts of pop, should not only be tolerated but in fact encouraged as part of the pageantry.

Following the *Movietone News* and the same cartoon as yesterday, *Thunder Birds* began and reprising what the Coleman boys did a day earlier, they all began searching the introductory scenes for Jonathan and Joseph. There they were again: marching wearing the same flight jackets that Thomas had worn yesterday (Joseph's) and today (Jonathan's). Today the older boys were prepared for their brief appearance in this scene and Jonathan spotted himself this time. Both boys loudly pointed themselves out on the screen, and the three dozen or so other patrons all turned to see what the commotion was coming from the row that housed the Colemans.

As the initial scenes in which the boys had appearances faded into the contrived plot, Jonathan found his mind fixated upon tonight's scheduled date with Francine and his early morning conversation with his father. Several times Thomas nudged his oldest brother to ask him a question about the plot or something about Thunderbird Field in real life, and Jonathan's initial response each time was a distracted "huh?" His mind was clearly somewhere else and both Gerald and Joseph knew where...and why.

Charlene, for her part, projected herself onscreen, playing Gene Tierney's role: the "dame" caught between two suitors: the English doctor-turned-would-be-flyer, and the man from her past trying to turn that Brit into a fully qualified pilot...and who of course also just happened to have been a close friend of the young Englishman's father during the previous war. How delicious it all would be! Playing – living – roles such as this one that would be shown over and over on screens all across the country, indeed all across the world, that people would fondly recall for years!

Irene Coleman occasionally peeked above Ruthie's head at her older daughter and could almost read

Charlene's thoughts as she watched her daughter enraptured by what she saw onscreen. Irene made up her mind that before the week was out she would get to the bottom of this Hollywood nonsense.

The movie concluded, the Colemans filed out of the theater. Despite the cheesy ending, the thrill of catching brief glimpses of Jonathan and Joseph up on the Senator's screen had indeed been the highlight of the outing. Just as after yesterday's showing, Thomas wanted to shout to one and all: "Hey! My brothers, both of them right here, were in that movie we all just saw!" His gloom from Sunday afternoon and evening had vanished...not forever, Gerald thought to himself as he looked over at the beaming Tommy, chattering with his brothers about the real-life counterpart to what they had just watched; but at least for a while the youngest boy had been yanked out of his gloomy mood.

They all paused in the lobby to once again don their winter clothes. Irene happened to look to her left and her eyes landed on a poster for the feature movie that would be starting next week after *Thunder Birds* completed its run: a new Judy Garland picture called *For Me and My Gal.* Her eyes traveled down the poster underneath the film's name where Judy Garland's co-stars were named. It was the second name that caught her eye. A familiar name; at least in the past two days.

Irene Coleman immediately looked to her right where Charlene was buttoning up her coat, and saw that her daughter was also staring at the name "Gene Kelly." Charlene, sensing that her mother was now staring at her, quickly looked at Irene and the two locked eyes.

Charlene now knew that her mother knew.

*   *   *

They all boarded the streetcar back to Polish Hill, though Charlene continued on to East Liberty and Peabody High for the afternoon's rehearsals. As Irene Coleman departed behind the others, she turned back to Charlene, looked her squarely in the eye, and sternly said:

"Come right home, I want to talk to you before dinner."

Charlene just nodded quickly and turned away from her mother. Her mind flashed back to that Christmas Day showdown with her mother. She could almost hear her mother's opening salvo all from last year over again: "I understand you're engaged." This year's version would likely be: "I understand you've been meeting with some actor."

Charlene forced the unpleasant thoughts from her head as the streetcar got underway. She needed to concentrate on getting her mind ready for rehearsals. The splendid, eager anticipation of today's rehearsal she had felt only hours earlier was now enveloped in the gathering storm clouds of the inevitable confrontation with her mother, but she did the best she could to focus on the music and the words and the choreography of each of her numbers.

While Charlene continued along, the rest of the family trooped from the streetcar stop to the house. Lunch was next on the agenda, and Irene was barely inside the front door before she headed straight into the kitchen to begin preparing the early afternoon meal for her family. Fortunately, today's lunch was especially easy and quick to prepare: liverwurst sandwiches with potato chips. Several months earlier the War Production Board had declared potato chips to be an "essential food," meaning that plants run by Wise, Jay's, and other food manufacturers were permitted to remain open and producing potato chips for civilian consumption. With winter around the corner and Victory Gardens out of business until next spring, plus canned vegetables mostly headed overseas to soldiers and sailors, potato chips were for the most part one of the only vegetables families such as Irene's would see on their plates. So Irene made sure to save enough ration stamps for Wise potato chips in particular (that brand being the Coleman family's favorite) or, in the absence of Wise chips on the market shelves, any other brand she could greedily procure.

Lunch was a hurried affair this day, despite not one of the family members having anything in particular to do or any place to be this afternoon (save Charlene, of course). The sandwiches were wolfed down – Jonathan and Joseph leading the way, eating almost as fast as if they were back at Thunderbird Field – and then Gerald and his sons parked themselves in the living room in time to catch the 2:00 news on NBC Red (technically just called plain "NBC" now since September, but everyone was so used to the "NBC Red" name they still used it without fail).

In Chicago, it was announced, three German-American men were sentenced to death for treason and each of their wives had been given sentences of 25 years, all for aiding one of the now-executed Nazi spies who had been secretly landed in the U.S. by U-Boat back in June. Four of the sentenced traitors were the parents, aunt, and uncle of one of the U-Boat spies. The NBC news announcer echoed the Judge's pronouncement of the "unholiness" of their treason and then served up a warning to other German-Americans contemplating such traitorous activities.

Secretary of the Navy Knox was quoted as proclaiming that the Marines had cut off the remaining Japanese on Guadalcanal from reinforcements and that "wiping out" the Japanese on the island was the Navy's objective.

News from North Africa; from Stalingrad, where a major tank battle was raging; and New Guinea followed before being followed by a commercial break for Chesterfields and then a War Board reminder urging "additional restraint" for this Thanksgiving holiday to aid the war effort, even beyond the imposed limitations of the rationing they all endured. Finally, the news gave way to the orchestra of Glenn Miller, who was now an Army Air Forces officer just as Jonathan and Joseph themselves would soon be.

The thunk of the afternoon *Pittsburgh Press* bouncing off of the front screen door after being tossed by the paperboy pulled Thomas from his chair to retrieve the paper. He brought the *Press* back inside and began to hand it to his father; an unusual act for many months now with his Pa working at the war plant almost every single day and then at his shop on Saturday to make up for the time spent away from his small business, and therefore rarely home when the afternoon *Press* arrived at the Coleman home.

"Give it to Joseph," Gerald countered though, shaking his head as Thomas tried to hand him the paper. "Let him and Jonathan see the paper while they're home, I'm sure they miss reading about the Pirates and the Hornets."

Thomas wheeled around and handed the newspaper instead to Joseph, who responded with a quick "Thanks, Tommy" as he gazed at the headlines that were mostly what they had just heard on NBC Red. He was about to pass the paper to Jonathan when, after flipping it over, his eyes landed on one of the smaller story headlines near the bottom:

Half of Jews in Poland Doomed by Hitler Axman

Above the headline, in smaller italicized print, the paper had added "*Exile Government Charges –*" to indicate that the report had come from Poland's government-in-exile and could well be anti-Nazi propaganda of some sort. Still, the first paragraph was chilling, claiming that Heinrich Himmler himself had ordered half of the Jewish population in occupied Poland to be executed by the end of the year! That couldn't be, Joseph immediately thought as he read on; how could the Nazis kill a million or more people in the five weeks left in 1942? They might want to, but was that even possible?

Regardless of the feasibility – or not – of killing that many poor victims, the details in the paragraphs that followed horrified Joseph as he read on. Old men and women herded to cemeteries where they were executed by firing squads; others packed into freight cars and transported off to "undisclosed points for liquidation."

Joseph handed the paper to Jonathan and pointed to the beginning of the article at the bottom of the front page. Jonathan quickly scanned the terrible paragraphs and his reaction was the same as Joseph's. Not that any of this was a surprise; the Nazis had been terrorizing and murdering Jews in their conquered countries as well as Germany itself since before America had been dragged into this war. Still, seeing the claimed number of intended victims in black and white newsprint was horrifyingly sobering.

"What are you looking at?" Thomas asked Jonathan, taking note that Joseph had pointed out a specific article in the *Press*.

Jonathan hesitated for a moment. Surely Thomas was aware of the panorama of the Nazis' horrible acts, but this blunt statement that more than a million people were targeted for execution…and there was nothing that America or Britain or Russia could do in time to save these poor souls?

Jonathan handed the paper to Thomas anyway; he might be only fifteen years old but he also might as well be aware of the reason, or at least one of the reasons, every aspect of their lives had been turned upside down as the nation had gone to war over the past year.

Thomas glanced at the same article his brothers had previously viewed and both Jonathan and Joseph watched the horror creep into the youngster's eyes as he read. As he finished the portion at the bottom of front page and flipped to find the continuation of the story inside, he looked over at Joseph first and then Jonathan.

"They're really doing all of this?" he said. His words weren't skeptical; rather they were "hopeful" in a way…hopeful that perhaps these proclaimed horrors were really just part of a propaganda campaign to demonize the Nazis as part of the war effort. Not that the Nazis needed any additional demonizing, of course; the horrors they had perpetrated were well-documented to one and all, over in Europe as well as here in America.

Both of his brothers nodded in unison, each one tightening his lips as he did so; that "yeah, unfortunately" response. Thomas looked over at his father, who did the same. The boy just sadly shrugged as he dropped the paper onto the end table before slumping back into his chair.

Gerald watched Thomas' reaction and then looked over at his other sons. The distinction between the war his sons were about to join and the one that he himself had participated in more than twenty years earlier, albeit on the periphery, was clearer than ever despite the enemy – Germany – being the same. It didn't matter that one or both of his elder sons could wind up fighting the Japanese instead of the Nazis; the horrors that Tojo's forces had perpetrated on villages and cities across China since the late '30s, and the brutal acts they had inflicted on civilians in the Philippines and Singapore and elsewhere since their coordinated attacks across the Pacific early last December, made them no different than Nazi Germany.

Back in '17 and '18, the Germany that America had fought had been a belligerent, bullying military power and had certainly provoked the United States into joining forces with the Allies through their U-Boat attacks on American merchant ships. And the Kaiser's regime, in many ways, had been a predecessor to Hitler's expansionist desires and had perpetrated atrocities of their own. Still, that war had primarily been the latest incarnation of centuries-old European conflicts over territory and wealth in which nearly every country on the continent had participated time and again. One could almost imagine those on Germany's side of the war believing in the "rightness" of their cause as they fought on during the Great War.

This time, though, there was no doubt in Gerald Coleman's mind that this was a battle against the vilest evils one could imagine. Any war is brutal, but the sheer scale of the horrors that the Nazis – as well as Tojo – continued to callously inflict on the world had to be halted. America had done its best to stay out of the fighting and support the English and the Russians in their fight, but now that they were in this war, it truly was a fight to the finish. Either "right" would win, or evil would; one side would crush the other into near-oblivion. There could be no negotiated cessation of hostilities that would come from this war as had happened the last time.

As he looked over at his two Air Corps sons, Gerald again realized that despite the fear that one or both of them could wind up losing his life in this war, what they would soon be doing was an absolute necessity. This tale told by the *Pittsburgh Press* article was only the most recent accentuation of this point, but having his sons home and sitting right before his very eyes, each shaking his head while reading about blatant intended Nazi horrors, helped stiffen Gerald Coleman's own resolve. He was doing his own small part in the war plant, as much as a man of his advancing years might do, and they would do theirs. And if it would be God's will that the war would last as long as Gerald expected it to, so would Tommy.

Gerald blew out a deep breath, and all three of his sons looked at him as he did.

"Boys," he said, "It's going to be a long war."

Jonathan, for his part, was thinking about the boys at *J. Weisberg & Sons* – the old man's sons – he used to work with who were now all scattered to Army, Navy, and Marines. He tried to imagine what it must be like for them, or for any of the other Jewish boys he knew and played football and baseball with at Schenley, to be fighting in this war knowing that maybe you had relatives still over in Europe who may very well be murdered by the Nazis. He wondered if they would fight with grim resolve to either save their relatives who might still be alive or avenge the terrible deaths of those who were not. He didn't know for certain but imagined that might well be the case.

"Boys," Gerald's voice interrupted Jonathan's somber thoughts, "you should go outside and throw the football around for a while. I think I'm going to enjoy a little snooze, seeing that it feels like a Sunday with me being home in the afternoon."

An uncoordinated chorus of staggered "okay, Pop" responses came from each of the Coleman boys as they all rose from their seats. Thomas went upstairs to grab his football while the older sons headed to the hall closet to grab their flight jackets.

"I'll let Tommy wear mine again," Joseph said to his brother, who just nodded in response before looking at his father.

"You sure, Pop? You don't want us to stay inside with you?"

Gerald shook his head.

"No, I'm feeling tired," he replied. "I could use a good snooze for an hour or so."

Gerald looked at Joseph and then back at Jonathan.

"Come back in after an hour and we'll have some more time to talk and listen to the radio before your Ma puts dinner on the table."

"Okay, Pop," they both replied, this time in absolutely perfect vocal unison as if they were offering a "Yes, sir!" response in formation out at Thunderbird Field.

*　　*　　*

"Smoke?"

Marty Walker looked over at the sailor who had approached him, a pack of smokes extended, as Marty stood by the coffee pot in the radioman's mess. Marty was just about to head outside on deck to get some air but decided that a smoke was in order. None of them could smoke out on deck, of course; even the faintest glow of a cigarette might be observed by a nearby U-Boat and be the trigger that would send them all to a watery grave. Not a single one of them would dare defy this order, even though enjoying a cigarette while bundled up under the chilly North Atlantic night air was just what almost every sailor aboard craved.

Marty reached for an Old Gold from the sailor's pack as he fished in his own pocket for a pack of matches. As he did he tried to remember the sailor's name. O'Shannon, he thought it was; a gunner. He didn't know the guy all that well even though they had sailed halfway around the world, been through *Operation Torch* together, and now were two-thirds of the way back from the coast of Morocco to Bermuda. Of the more than 1,000 sailors and officers on board the *Augusta*, Marty could safely say he knew about a hundred of them fairly well and another two hundred or so, sailors like O'Shannon here, by sight and maybe – with a little bit of struggle – by name. For a moment he wondered why O'Shannon was in the small radioman's mess, seeing that he was a gunner on the ship, but ever since the *Augusta* had pulled away from North Africa, sailors were feeling a little bit more at ease and wandering into different parts of the ship than their usual ones when they had been at General Quarters during *Torch* and its buildup.

The two sailors puffed in silence, finishing their smokes in little more than five minutes.

"I'm going up," Marty said as he crushed out his cigarette butt. "Wanna grab some air?"

"Sure," O'Shannon replied. Marty studied the boy for another brief moment before the two of them headed out into the night. O'Shannon appeared to be about the same age as Marty, with a babyish face.

The two walked out into the night air. As he had done every night he had been on deck since the *Augusta* had left North Africa, Marty paused to take in the endless field of stars. The peaceful vastness, the sheer beauty, contrasted so very much with the smoky clamor and manic bustle when the ship had been off the coast of North Africa during *Torch*.

"So where ya from?" O'Shannon's questions interrupted Marty's thoughts.

"Pittsburgh. You?"

"Brooklyn," came the reply.

"Dodgers fan, yeah?" Marty asked, knowing the answer.

O'Shannon grinned.

"You know it," he replied. "I was at all three of the World Series games at Ebbets Field last year. Guess it don't matter that the Dodgers didn't get back this year, seein' that we were out here and I wasn't gonna be there anyway to watch, right?"

"I guess," Marty replied. His own Pittsburgh Pirates hadn't been to a World Series since way back in '27, when they lost four straight games to Babe Ruth and Lou Gehrig and their Murderers' Row Yankee teammates. Marty was only four years old then and didn't remember any of it. He envied O'Shannon here actually going to a real World Series game – three of them, nonetheless! – not just listening to the Series on the radio.

"So you got any brothers also in the war?" O'Shannon continued.

Marty shook his head.

"Nah. My little brother Calvin is only eleven, and I have a sister Lorraine who is sixteen. My two cousins are Air Corps cadets in Arizona right now, though. They should be finishing up soon but I don't know what they'll be flying or where they're headed."

"My brother Billy is a bombardier on a B-17 in England," O'Shannon replied. "Maybe your brothers and my brother will wind up flying together, ya know?"

Marty shrugged.

"I guess," he answered, thinking that with the hundreds of thousands, maybe even millions, of flyers who would eventually be in the Army Air Forces the odds of that happening were pretty remote...but you never know, stranger things had happened.

"I got another brother Tommy who's an Army corporal in New Guinea," O'Shannon continued. "And then Patrick is back in North Africa with Patton."

"So four of you in all in the service?"

"Yeah," O'Shannon nodded. "My Ma and Pa must be goin' through a rough time back in Brooklyn; you know, worrying about all of us."

"Any others in your family?"

"I got three sisters and one more younger brother, Michael, he's fifteen now."

"My other cousin Tommy is fifteen," Marty replied. "I guess if this lasts long enough they'll both be joining up around the same time, huh?"

"Yeah," O'Shannon replied. "I guess they would be."

The two paused for a couple minutes.

"You know what's a strange feeling?" O'Shannon finally broke the silence.

"Huh?" Marty answered.

It took another moment for O'Shannon to continue.

"Right now, back there" – O'Shannon nodded in the direction of North Africa, where the *Augusta* had been a few days earlier – "Patrick could have been killed five minutes ago, or maybe yesterday, and I wouldn't know he was dead maybe for weeks."

He paused again, then looked at Marty before continuing.

"You know what I mean? Back home, if something happened to Patrick someone would come up to our flat to let us know right away, or maybe by the next morning at the latest. But some Nazi could have shot him dead an hour ago and my Ma and Pa might not find out for a week or two; maybe longer. And I might not find out for another week or two or even longer after that."

O'Shannon looked out at the blackness of the North Atlantic where the horizon was barely visible in the distance, then back at Marty.

"Same with Billy. His plane might get shot down but we might never find out if he's alive and in a Nazi prisoner camp or dead until the war is over."

Marty thought about what O'Shannon was saying.

"It's a strange feeling," O'Shannon went on. "All four of us are scattered all over the world right now and if one of us gets killed, by the time everyone back home and the rest of us find out so much time will have passed that it's…I don't know, I can't really explain it. But it's strange, ya know?"

Marty nodded.

"I get it," he replied. "I don't got no brothers in the war like you do but my cousins and I are pretty close. During the Depression we lived in their house for about six years so they are like my own brothers. But yeah, if Jonathan were to get shot down on a bombing raid it might be a long time until I got word, especially if we're in the middle of something like *Torch* with no mail or restricted service. We'd get into port one day and our mail would catch up with us and we'd get letters written a couple months earlier, and I might find out that way. So all that time I woulda thought he was alive but he actually was dead."

Marty was about to add "Or suppose a U-Boat were to hit us with a torpedo right now and sink us; my folks might not know until Christmas" but thought better of uttering those words. Just the very thought of dying that way made him physically ill, and Marty was superstitious enough to believe that refusing to voice that thought would help keep that horrible event from occurring.

"So they got a great Thanksgiving planned for us, huh?" Marty said, desperate to change the subject.

"Yeah, I guess," O'Shannon replied morosely. Obviously the boy was preoccupied with worry about his brothers' safety. I guess in this case I'm glad I don't have any brothers old enough yet to be in this thing, Marty thought to himself. He was terribly homesick and hated what he had just gone through; even being on the periphery of the fighting as a Navy radioman was causing him terrifying nightmares almost every time he tried to catch some sleep. But at least he only worried about himself, at least for now. Once Jonathan and Joseph started flying missions over Europe or out in the Pacific, wherever they wound up, he could see himself feeling much the same as O'Shannon did; having that constant undercurrent of worry for his cousins' safety as well as his own.

"Come on," Marty elbowed O'Shannon. The chills that were causing him to shiver so badly were only partly caused by the cold North Atlantic night, but regardless he thought another cup of steaming hot coffee back in the mess was just the thing that he – and this other sailor – really, *really* needed at the moment.

*   *   *

This was turning out to be Charlene Coleman's worst rehearsal ever!

Fumbling words...doing her dance steps out of order...even bumping into Sammy Canter twice as she "zigged when she should have zagged." *Everyone* was staring at her, wondering what in the world had gotten into her since last Friday. The whispers began among those watching Charlene:

"Her brothers are home from Air Corps training; maybe something happened to one of them?"

"Maybe she has a big head from Gene Kelly saying nice things to her last Friday, and she isn't concentrating..."

"Maybe she has another new boyfriend and her brain just emptied out..."

The show's director, Mrs. Phillips, finally halted Charlene's and Sammy's near-mockery of *I Could Write a Book*.

"Let's take five, everybody," Mrs. Phillips said, and then wagged a "come over here" finger at Charlene before she could slink off the stage.

"What's the matter today, honey?" Mrs. Phillips said soothingly to Charlene. She was the music teacher at Taylor-Allderdice High School; a plump, pleasant-demeanored, gray-haired woman a little bit older than Charlene's mother, who was well aware of the fragileness of the confidence of a high school girl...even a very talented one such as Charlene Coleman.

"I don't know," Charlene said quietly, her eyes downcast.

"Charlene?" Her tones demanded an answer, but still the girl would offer nothing.

"Charlene," Mrs. Phillips continued, "everyone has a rehearsal day where nothing works right. Sometimes your mind gets distracted with problems, or sometimes it just seems that you've forgotten everything that you've learned and always do so well. This is true even for the very best performers, like you."

At "like you" Charlene finally raised her head to look directly at Mrs. Phillips, who continued.

"You're very good, Charlene; but then again you know that. You're got the best voice in the entire show, and you are one of the best dancers. Didn't Mister Gene Kelly himself say that to you last Friday?"

The girl's face darkened immediately; a combination of blushing and trepidation.

"Ah," Mrs. Phillips said upon watching Charlene's reaction, "this is something to do with Mister Kelly, I see."

Charlene immediately shook her head but Mrs. Phillips wasn't fooled. For a flash of an instant Mrs. Phillips was worried that based on Charlene's reaction some sort of impropriety may have happened between the girl and the Broadway dancer, but she dismissed that thought as quickly as it came into her head. She knew Mister Kelly well enough from having taken tap dance classes herself at his Squirrel Hill dance studio up until the time five years earlier that he headed to New York to make a name for himself. He was an upstanding Pittsburgh boy and when he had greeted Mrs. Phillips so warmly the previous Friday before rehearsals over at Peabody, he had gushed more about his new bride than his smashing success in *Pal Joey* or his first movie role in the Judy Garland picture that was about to open next week. He would be the last person to dally behind his new wife's back with a young high school girl such as Charlene.

It took a few more moments but eventually Mrs. Phillips pulled the truth from Charlene.

"But you haven't even spoken with your mother yet, am I right?" she asked after Charlene finished blurting out what her mother had apparently discovered and her fears of the impending showdown this afternoon.

"No," Charlene replied quietly.

"Well, first of all," Mrs. Phillips said, "despite what Mister Gene Kelly may have said, you don't just waltz out to Hollywood, show up at Metro Goldwyn, and say 'hello, here I am!' Look at Mister Kelly himself."

She proceeded to tell Charlene what she knew of Gene Kelly's long journey from local dance studio instructor to his first unsuccessful attempt at landing on Broadway; his brief return to Pittsburgh before going back to New York and finally landing a Broadway role; and then finally winning his breakthrough role in *The Time of Your Life*.

"I'm sure Mister Kelly didn't mean to imply that if you were able to go out to Hollywood right now, Mister Goldwyn would immediately sign you up for a starring role in a new musical…"

"But my mother will *never* let me do any of this now!" Charlene interrupted, almost in tears.

"Let me talk to your mother," Mrs. Phillips said. "You have plenty of time and you need to finish high school first anyway. Mister Gene Kelly and MGM and Clark Gable and all the rest of them will still be there waiting in six months or a year or two years; I promise you."

Charlene skeptically replied with a muttered "okay." Mrs. Phillips obviously had little or no experience facing off against the iron will of Irene Coleman, Charlene thought to herself; that was almost for certain. As of two or three hours ago, Charlene Coleman's aspirations for artistic fame had been crushed for good; of *that* she *was* certain.

"Here's what we'll do," Mrs. Phillips continued, then lowered her voice conspiratorially. "Let's focus on getting you back on track; singing and dancing better than anyone else in the entire show, and then ask your mother to come watch you tomorrow afternoon when we'll be over at Schenley. Don't tell her that I would like to talk with her, just tell her that you would like her to watch you sing and dance so she can see how much you love it and how good you are. And then we can see how things go. Okay?"

Charlene's mood began to brighten…at least a little bit.

"Okay," she replied, still skeptical that anything Mrs. Phillips or Gene Kelly or even Franklin Delano Roosevelt himself might say to Irene Coleman could convince her that Charlene's new aspirations were something to be taken seriously, not dismissed as the fanciful flightiness of a young high school girl.

Mrs. Phillips allowed an extra five minutes of break time to allow Charlene to take a short pause herself, and then with her pleasant-toned – but commanding – voice called the young troop back together for a run-through from the top. This time, when Charlene and Sammy performed *I Could Write a Book* they were much better than earlier, though still not as good as the previous Friday. However there were no more collisions due to missed dance steps, and Charlene's tones were crisper and sharper than they had been before the break.

Then, when it was time for Charlene's solo of *Bewitched, Bothered, and Bewildered*, she was even stronger. During the first verse she snuck a glance at Mrs. Phillips who beamed back approvingly. From that point on, the looming confrontation with Irene Coleman was mostly put out of Charlene's mind…at least until Tuesday's rehearsal was completed and Charlene boarded the streetcar for the long, long (or so it seemed) ride home and the apprehension of the impending confrontation forced itself front and center in Charlene's thoughts once again.

*　　*　　*

Irene Coleman had already decided that her "discussion" with her daughter would occur after dinner, not before. She knew that Jonathan and Joseph wanted to be on their way for their dates and frankly, stewing at the thought of Jonathan walking out the front door to embark on a date with Francine Donner after *everything* that had happened would be just the thing to work her up into a mood for setting her daughter straight.

Jonathan had spilled the beans an hour earlier, walking into Irene's kitchen as she was finishing up the preparations for tonight's dinner of wartime meatloaf. Just as during the Depression, Irene's meatloaf was far more "loaf" than "meat" with plenty of filling. For much of the past summer after her sons had departed for Arizona, the Coleman family dinners had been meatless most evenings due to rationing. However, while her sons were home this week Irene had vowed that even beyond the Sunday and Thursday feasts she would prepare the best dinners she could and include meat in every one of them.

Irene had listened in silence as Jonathan blurted out that he and Joseph were going to the movies with Francine and one of her friends. He had finished his reticent monologue with "It's okay, Ma; I know what I'm doing" and Irene had simply looked at him and replied, "I hope so" before turning back to her meal preparation. Considering what that hussy had done to her son last year, she couldn't understand why in the world he would want to go out on a date with her; but then again, who could say what was in the mind of her son. Anyway, her more immediate concern was her daughter's foolery; if anything were to brew with Jonathan and Francine she would deal with it, perhaps even put a stop to it, later on.

The mood at the Coleman dinner table that night was strained. Even Ruthie picked up on the various unspoken subplots, and she kept her eyes downcast at her plate as she ate. There was only a little bit of conversation, and most of it revolved around the boys' cameo appearances in

Thunder Birds and what they had all watched earlier in the day.

Shortly after 6:00, as Gerald settled into his easy chair and flicked on the NBC Red news program, Jonathan and Joseph headed upstairs to wash up and put on fresh shirts for their dates. No uniforms tonight; civies instead. They reappeared downstairs twenty minutes later, went into the kitchen to tell their mother they were leaving, and then did the same to their Pa as they headed out the front door. Gerald locked eyes with Jonathan as they walked by and then his own gaze traveled down to glimpse Jonathan's left hand buried deep in his left front pants pocket. He knew exactly what Jonathan was doing: clasping his Morgan dollar talisman, as if desperate to draw the will and sustenance he would need for this reuniting date with his would-have-been fiancé. Now that the moment was here, no doubt Jonathan was wondering to himself just exactly what he had gotten himself into and what he might be in store for this evening. Would there be an angry exchange of words and accusations? Would there be a friendly, or even bittersweet, final parting between the two of them? Or might the calendar be turned back, as if controlled by one of those fantasy time machines, to the point at which the two of them...

"See you later, Pop," Joseph's cheery tones interrupted Gerald's musings about his oldest boy. Ah, to be a young man in Joseph's shoes this very evening. For a fleeting instant, Gerald Coleman was envious of his middle son. Whereas Jonathan's date this evening was one that came encumbered by a long history and significant complications, Joseph was in the throes of that splendid feeling that envelops a young man when he is about to go on that very first date with a girl he fancies. Quite possibly the evening could end with Joseph and this girl Angie – no, it's Abby, Gerald corrected his own thoughts – finding they have nothing in common, or it could well be that first date when a boy finds he's suddenly falling head over heals for a young woman.

Suddenly Gerald was enveloped in sadness; far more for Joseph than for Jonathan. Suppose that Joseph had indeed just met the girl of his dreams; that special young woman who, on that first date, he decides has everything he could ever want in a wife? Then what? Within days he would be on a train back to Arizona and other than – hopefully – a brief furlough back home between finishing flight training and shipping out overseas, he would have no chance at all to nurture anything that might develop with this girl.

What a cruel trick of fate! Jonathan, at least, had a history with Francine. If somehow, some way, the two of them were to patch up what had happened last year and put it behind them, it wasn't out the question that they might enter into a very sudden engagement as he and Jonathan had briefly mused over this very morning. Or maybe an engagement would happen in six or nine months if and when Jonathan returned home for that final furlough before going off to war. Either was possible; perhaps even likely.

But Joseph? Gerald saw no way that the poor boy would ever have a future with this girl, at least until after the war. Quite possibly in two or three or four years Joseph would return home (Gerald automatically found his right hand knocking against the wooden armrest on his easy chair) and this Abby would still be unmarried; and at that time they could pick up where they would leave off tonight and perhaps tomorrow night and see where things wound up. But by that time the girl would be twenty or twenty-one or even older, and quite possibly already married and a mother. Gerald had a hunch young girls might be waiting a bit longer to get married while the war was on, especially with so many of the boys over in Europe and the Pacific, but one could never tell; the lure of becoming a wife and a mother was always a powerful one and if the girl was as pretty and sweet as Jonathan said she was when Gerald surreptitiously asked his oldest son about Joseph's date, she may well be snapped up before Joseph ever set foot back in Pittsburgh.

Ah well, Gerald sighed; there was nothing that he could do about the situation other than be there for Joseph to talk to if the boy needed. He watched his sons depart and then settled in for an evening of listening to the radio; mostly marking time until *Fibber McGee & Molly* came on at 9:30 Eastern War Time. He might well be snoozing afterwards as Bob Hope's program and then Red Skelton's played, but he was determined to stay put in the living room until at least 11:00 in case his boys came back early by then and wanted to talk with him about...well, about anything.

$$* \quad * \quad *$$

In the kitchen Irene, Charlene, and Ruthie were washing and drying dishes, tableware, pots, and pans...mostly in silence. When they were almost done, Irene turned to her youngest and said,

"Ruthie, go up to your room and play for a while." She tried to issue her command in as pleasant of a voice as she could, but Ruthie wasn't fooled; she just nervously looked at her mother for a couple of seconds and then wordlessly left the kitchen.

After a few more seconds, Irene looked at Charlene and commanded:

"Tell me about this Mister Gene Kelly."

While her mother's words weren't exactly as she had predicted earlier in the day, her expectation for what Irene Coleman's opening barrage would be was right on the mark.

"He's a Broadway star who's from Pittsburgh, Ma," Charlene responded with her rehearsed rebuttal. "He came up to me after rehearsals on Friday and told me that he thought I was one of the best singers he had ever seen and thought I was good enough to be in the movies." As she continued explaining, Charlene's voice gained more confidence with every single word. By the end of her rebuttal, Charlene fully believed exactly what she was conveying to her mother: that she *was* a fantastic singer and *was* good enough to be in the movies. So take that!

"I see," Irene Coleman nodded when Charlene had finished, those two words slightly tinged with a mixture of sarcasm and skepticism. "So you think that now you will be quitting school and going out to Hollywood with this Mister Gene Kelly to become a big movie star, like Judy Garland?"

"I never said that!" Now Charlene was angry. "I *never* said anything about quitting school! I'm almost done, anyway! I'll be in the Pearl Harbor benefit in a couple of weeks and then maybe I will get into a show at the Pittsburgh Playhouse after New Year's – that's where Gene Kelly started, you know – and then…"

"Ah," Irene Coleman interrupted. "My daughter wants to be a big star and keep company with Clark Gable and Lana Turner and…"

It was Charlene's turn to interrupt.

"I never said that, *you* did!" She was as close to yelling at her mother as she might ever get. In the living room Gerald Coleman, as well as Thomas – who had joined his father – heard the commotion above the radio and looked at each other. Gerald just shook his head a couple of times, that "just leave it alone, it's not for us" gesture, and went back to scanning the rest of that afternoon's *Pittsburgh Press* he hadn't read earlier.

"I *love* singing and dancing!" Charlene was wound up. If she stopped and thought about it for a moment, she would be forced to admit she was indeed enamored with the thought of being a sought-after movie star; thus her fantasized photo shoot in her bedroom this very morning, as well as her consternation over whether or not she might have to change her name to something more "star-like." But first and foremost, she had become enraptured not only with the act itself of performing but also the glorious, self-satisfying feeling of having progressed so far and so quickly. Having Mrs. Phillips and even a Broadway star like Gene Kelly affirm that Charlene's feelings about her own skills were indeed on the mark was the icing on the cake. And knowing that maybe, just maybe, singing and dancing – and acting – might be in her future had given Charlene a wondrous feeling all weekend long.

And there was no way she was going to let her mother ruin that feeling!

The two argued back and forth for another five minutes. Point; counterpoint. Argument; counter-argument. Irene abandoned the sarcastic, belittling overtones that weren't her usual style anyway; even as she argued with her daughter a part of her mind had gone to work trying to figure out exactly why she had reacted that way.

"Mrs. Phillips – she's the show's director – told me to ask you to come to rehearsals tomorrow at Allderdice to watch me," Charlene finally threw out, totally forgetting Mrs. Phillips' instructions not to relate that particular detail to her mother. Charlene's voice calmed a little bit. "She thinks I'm just wonderful; as good as Gene Kelly said I am. She says that I can get started by joining a show at the Pittsburgh Playhouse first and then I can…"

"You will do no such thing," Irene Coleman interrupted. "It's a good thing that you do this singing and dancing while you are in high school and maybe if we can afford to send you to Mount Mercy you can do more of it while you are in college. But you're going to be eighteen very soon and graduating from high school and you should start thinking about…"

Again, Charlene's turn to interrupt.

"Thinking about what?" Charlene was almost yelling again. "Getting married? Is that all you want me to do? You weren't very happy last year when you found out that I wanted to get married to Larry, and you did everything you could to put a stop to that!"

"You were only sixteen years old then!" Irene rebutted, her voice also raised. "And look what happened; that boy disappeared just like I said he would, didn't he?"

Irene shifted gears.

"I only want what's best for you," she said, trying to make her words as soothing as she could. "Even if you wait until you're done with high school to go to Hollywood or New York or somewhere else you know that it's a hard life and people aren't very nice to you. You go and try out for a show or a movie but so do hundreds of other pretty girls who also can sing and dance. Maybe not as well as you, but you will probably have to keep trying and trying and there are no guarantees that you'll get chosen for parts. And some of those other girls will...will...they'll do things to make sure they get those parts even if you're a better singer or dancer..."

Irene paused for a brief moment before continuing.

"Don't you want to have a nice, safe life without all of that disappointment? Don't you want to..."

Charlene interrupted, this time tears instantly springing to her eyes.

"There is no such thing anymore as a 'nice, safe life!' Don't you understand? The entire world is falling apart around us! Jonathan and Joseph are going off to war! Don't you think they would both like to be back here in Pittsburgh with a 'nice, safe life?' *Everything* has changed! We might *never* have a 'nice, safe life' again with the war! Suppose the Nazis invade us? Suppose they start bombing us the way they bombed London? You keep talking about the world as it was last year, but it's gone! You want me to find some boy and get engaged and then married, and then have children...but that might never happen for *any* of us ever again! Why won't you just let me try to do something that I'm good at and that makes me happy? It may be my last chance!"

Irene was stunned into silence. She had presumed that her daughter's new-found fascination with this whole Hollywood and Broadway nonsense was solely a result of some huckster – this Mister Gene Kelly – encouraging a modestly talented young girl to pursue some foolish notion. Even if he didn't have any underhanded intentions towards this young girl, which apparently he didn't, he was simply egging on these ideas that would almost certainly cause Charlene a great deal of angst and pain as she faced one frustrating setback after another.

No doubt girlish foolishness was indeed part of Charlene's aspirations, but Irene simply hadn't even considered the desperate anxiety that Charlene felt in light of America being at war for almost an entire year. The newspapers might print their bold headlines proclaiming victories in battles but the reality was that years of war lay ahead for all of them. They might all relish the escapism of watching that contrived *Thunder Birds* movie that came with the added bonus of her two sons having small appearances, but they all knew – even though none could bear to speak the words – that Jonathan or Joseph, or both, might never come back alive from this war. Even if Charlene's doomsday scenario of Nazi invasions and bombings here on American soil never came true, there was plenty of fighting and dying ahead over in Europe and the Pacific for who knew how much longer to come. So even beyond her own sons' safety lay the ominous shadow of a sorrowfully changed life for all of them should the unspeakable happen.

Irene stood there, looking at her daughter. Flashes of her own younger years when she had had aspirations for a life of travel throughout Europe, Hong Kong, and other far-away destinations and the accompanying splendor were juxtaposed with images of her own daughter taking a bow after a splendid opening night Broadway performance (Irene and Gerald occupying choice seats in the audience that night, of course) or being bombarded by flashbulbs as photographers rushed to capture her picture following Charlene's latest starring role in a hit movie.

Then Irene endured several very brief – but extremely vivid – conjured snippets of the entire Coleman family, or what was left of the family, scraping through the rubbled ruins of Polish Hill that looked so much like a bombed-out English neighborhood during the Blitz. A horrifying image no doubt; and, God willing, an extremely unlikely one. But still a possibility, Irene conceded.

Irene sighed deeply. She wanted so much for her daughter to make a good life for herself but, she was forced to admit, Charlene was right: their world *had* been turned upside down, and yesterday's "good life" might very well not be a possible one in the years ahead. And even if America came out on the victorious side of this war, as they all prayed would be the case, there would be a tremendous toll paid over the next several years and perhaps for years afterwards. Was it really so wrong for Charlene Coleman to have adjusted to this new reality before her mother did, and for the girl to have decided to strive for a different life than the future that one and all had presumed she would follow before the world went to war?

Charlene sensed that her mother's stubborn position was weakening.

"Just come with me to rehearsals tomorrow," she said to her mother, her own voice calmer than it had been since this argument had begun…yet still carrying the occasional sob as her tears continued.

"Talk to Mrs. Phillips and listen to what she tells you about me."

No response from her mother.

"Okay?" Charlene persisted.

Irene Coleman shrugged her shoulders and nodded in resigned consent as she turned away.

* * *

"Back *again?*" the girl in the *Senator's* ticket booth said as she eyed Jonathan.

"You must *really* like this movie!" she continued, then looked over at Joseph.

"You too," she said to Joseph, smiling seductively at him despite Abby Sobol standing less than a foot away from him.

It took Jonathan a moment to realize that this girl must have recognized them from when they were here earlier today with the entire family, or perhaps yesterday when they had come with Tommy; or maybe both. He looked over at Francine, whose eyes were angrily blazing at the girl in the ticket booth. How dare she flirt with Jonathan when Francine was standing right there with him! And the same with Joseph, with Abby so obviously accompanying him as his date!

The ticket girl looked directly back at Francine and smiled sweetly; that "okay, he's yours *for now*" look that the worst of the hussies at Schenley used to give Francine while they still shamelessly tried to move in on Jonathan and steal him from her. Francine looked over at Abby, who was almost snarling at the ticket girl.

It doesn't matter, Francine thought to herself as Jonathan and Joseph each laid down a dollar for two of the tickets and the four of them headed inside the theater. She might have her eye on Jonathan – or on Joseph, for that matter – but the girl was stuck inside the ticket booth and there was no way in the world that she would sink her claws into either of them tonight...or for the rest of the couple of days they were still here. That thought immediately saddened Francine, though – the sudden remembrance that by dawn on Friday, Jonathan would be on a train headed back out west! – so she forced away any thoughts of Jonathan automatically escaping the clutches of this floozy ticket girl simply because his furlough would end.

Jonathan, for his part, was amused by Francine's blatant reaction to the ticket girl's flirting. Her reaction was so obviously genuine; not contrived in any way. She actually was jealous – apparently *very* jealous – that the pretty girl in the booth had not only noticed Jonathan at least once before but also gave no mind to the fact that Jonathan was showing up this time with a date.

And Abby Sobol was apparently having the same reaction when the girl shifted her attentions to Joseph; that was funny as well, considering this was her very first date with Joseph. Maybe it was simply that the ticket girl was attracted to the two of them because she could tell they were Air Corps flying cadets home on furlough; and that any two other Joes could have been standing in front of the ticket booth wearing A-2 flight jackets and she would have shown the same flirtatious interest. Still, Francine's and Abby's reactions were very revealing, each for their own set of reasons.

Once inside the lobby Jonathan offered Francine popcorn and pop but she declined, as did Abby when Joseph made the same offer. They all headed into the dimly lit theater. Despite the prime movie-watching evening hour, the theater was only about a quarter full; barely more people than were there yesterday when they came with Tommy. No doubt about it; *Thunder Birds* was nearing the end of its run here at the Senator at the right time. Maybe that Judy Garland picture for which Francine had pointed out the lobby poster would bring more customers into the theater next week.

Joseph cleared his throat as the four of them surveyed the seats from the aisle in the back of the theater.

"Um, we're going to go sit over there" – he nodded to his left, near the back of the theater – "okay?" Implicit in Joseph's "we're going to sit..." statement was an unspoken request to Jonathan that he and Francine should sit *anywhere* else except near where he and Abby would be seated. Jonathan involuntarily let out a small snort then caught himself. He was surprised that his brother was being so blatant in front of this girl on their very first date, but then it dawned on him that maybe sitting away from Francine and Jonathan was indeed Abby's idea. Maybe she was a faster girl than she seemed?

Or maybe, it suddenly occurred to him, that indeed it was Abby's idea but *not* because she wanted semi-privacy to neck with Joseph. Maybe Abby and Francine had conspired that the privacy should be afforded to Jonathan and Francine, and Abby had just enlisted Joseph to make this request so Francine wouldn't have to be put in the awkward position of doing so herself.

Whatever the reason, Joseph and Abby headed towards the back of the left section of the theater while Francine eyed three or four totally empty rows a little bit more forward but on the right side of the theater.

"Come on," she said as she lightly took Jonathan's arm. "Let's go sit over there, okay?"

As they walked in the direction Francine had indicated, Jonathan was walloped by wave after wave of dormant memories of past movies he and Francine had seen here or at the Strand or the Schenley. *Rebecca*, the first movie they ever saw together; *Pinocchio*; *The Philadelphia Story*; *The Shop*

Around the Corner...so many of them! So much time spent together!

"Tell me again about the scenes you are in," Francine said to Jonathan in lowered tones as they sat down just as it was time to stand again for The Star-Spangled Banner. Jonathan flashed a single index finger at her – wait a moment until this is over – and then, as they sat down and he removed his flight jacket as the *Movietone News* began, he told her which scenes to watch for.

The same news; the same cartoon...as the Hitleresque Big Bad Wolf was vanquished by the three little pigs (with the Wolf winding up in the fires of hell in the very last scene) Jonathan sat shoulder to shoulder with Francine...not holding hands with her, nor putting his left arm around her shoulders and pulling her in tight; just that pressing of shoulders against one another to hopefully banish any last-minute jitters either of them felt about this date after all that had happened and all the time that had passed.

Thunder Birds began, and Jonathan pointed out Joseph and himself in the first marching scene. Francine barely had time to react but when the classroom scene came on and Jonathan pointed himself out again, Francine gaped open-mouthed at the screen and as soon as the scene changed she looked over at Jonathan, astonished.

"Oh my God! That was you!" she said, her eyes wide open as she grasped Jonathan's left arm with both of her hands.

Jonathan shrugged.

"Just like Gary Cooper," he said nonchalantly but inside he was thrilled at Francine's reaction. For a fleeting instant he wondered if Abby Sobol was having the same reaction across the theater at the sight of Joseph on screen, and he was tempted to turn back and try to see if he could tell in the darkened theater. But the formation running scene they were both in was coming up shortly and besides, at the moment he really didn't care very much what Joseph and Abby were doing or saying. For all he knew, the two of them could be necking already! He dismissed that thought as soon as it occurred to him; that would mean that they would miss Joseph's on-screen appearances. After the cameos were finished and the movie's plot got going, though…

The formation running scene came and went and Francine grasped Jonathan's arm again at the sight of him, though not quite as eagerly as in the previous scene. There was obviously something about that one particular vision of him sitting in his khakis in an Air Corps classroom that had made her heart leap…

"Are there any more scenes with you and Joseph?" Francine leaned over to her right and whispered barely loudly enough for Jonathan to hear.

"Nah, that's it," he replied.

"Are you sure?" she whispered again.

"Um, yeah; pretty sure, we saw the movie twice in the past two days and didn't see ourselves at all again."

"Good."

With that single syllable Francine turned her entire body to her right, reached up with her left arm and put her hand on the back of Jonathan's head as he turned towards her in a natural response to her movements. She gently pulled his head towards her as her lips parted. For a split second Jonathan had the overwhelming urge to pull away but he fought through it as his lips met hers and they began to kiss.

*　　*　　*

Jonathan had thought through this possibility countless times over the past day after they had agreed to go see the movie this evening; the possibility that they would wind up kissing, maybe even necking, just like in times past when they were together as boyfriend and girlfriend. Each time Jonathan wondered if involuntarily conjured images of her kissing Donnie Yablonski popping into his brain at that very moment would cause him to recoil away from her. Talking to her, walking alongside her, even feeling the delicious electricity of her hand on top of his at the counter at Jack Canter's yesterday; acts like those seemed to have somehow been reborn, overcoming what had happened with her and Donnie.

But kissing her? The same as Donnie had done before he had...had... Jonathan honestly didn't know if he could actually kiss Francine if that moment arrived. Consequently he had firmly decided that he would *not* attempt to kiss her this evening except for maybe a goodnight peck when he saw her to her front door. He also had entertained the thought that if he tried to "make the moves" on Francine this evening, she herself might recoil away from him for her own reasons. Therefore, the safest course of all would be to avoid putting both of them in that position...at least for tonight.

Now, however, it was Francine who had initiated the kiss. Jonathan fought through the powerful urge to pull back away from her as her lips found his. Within a few seconds all of his worries had dissolved. She of course must have been kissing Donnie Yablonski before things went much farther between them but Jonathan suddenly had no doubt in his mind that any such kisses from Francine had been with her lips only, whereas she was now this very moment kissing Jonathan with her *heart*. As his mind formed this thought while the two of them sweetly, softly kissed each other he told himself that even though this idea was so corny it might as well be from one of those girl's novels that Charlene reads, Jonathan knew it to be the absolute truth.

*   *   *

Neither Francine nor Jonathan saw much of the movie. In Jonathan's case, he had already seen it three times in all; twice within the past 26 hours or so. After the first two or three minutes of kissing when they both came up for air, Francine asked Jonathan:

"Is this movie any good?"

He grinned.

"Truthfully, no," he replied.

"Good," she murmured as she leaned towards him once again and reached for his head to pull him towards her as well. A minute or so later Jonathan did break away for a brief instant and looked at Francine.

"Of course, there is my big love scene with Gene Tierney; don't you want to watch that?"

Francine chuckled.

"No," she said with a light laugh. "You're finished doing love scenes with her."

Just as they began to kiss again, she added:

"Or anyone else."

*   *   *

After leaving the Senator the four of them walked a couple blocks up Liberty Avenue to one of the coffee shops near Pennsylvania Station. Several times Jonathan looked down at Francine and caught her and Abby exchanging glances. "Girls communicating with each other with their eyes, they all do it." One of his more philosophical Schenley High buddies had once said something like that when a group of Jonathan's friends had been clustered one day in the stands adjoining the football field, talking about how to figure out if a girl was really ready for you to put the moves on her. His friend's observation had been that if any of your gal's girlfriends were with her, watch how they look back and forth at each other; if you pay close enough attention you'll be able to tell almost without fail what's in your girl's head even if she's not saying a word.

What Jonathan picked up from Abby's looks, not so much Francine's – he really couldn't see Francine's face that clearly since she would be looking away from him each time – was a "so now what?" sentiment. As in: "Okay, you've broken through the ice and necked for a long while in the movie, just like old times. So now what?"

The half hour or so the four of them spent in the booth at the coffee shop was a strained affair, though not because any of them was uncomfortable being around any of the others. Rather, it was if they all felt an obligation for a brief "time out" between what had occurred with each couple back in the darkened seats at the *Senator* and what might come next. But at the same time, all were impatient to move on to whatever lay ahead that night.

For Joseph and Abby, sparks had flown. Almost identical to what had happened with Jonathan and Francine, the moment the last of the scenes featuring cameos by the Colemans had passed, the two of them began kissing. In their case, though, it was Joseph who initiated that first kiss but Abby was certainly a willing participant. About halfway through the movie Joseph had finally summoned enough courage to begin to move his right hand upwards from her waist, but he had gotten no further than her midsection when Abby's hand had landed firmly on his and moved it back into safe territory. Secretly, Joseph was glad she had halted his advances; he had felt an obligation to make his move before the movie had concluded but he was quickly becoming more and more bewitched by this girl and secretly he was glad that he had learned so quickly she wasn't a "fast girl."

Coffee and pie finished all around, Jonathan passed around Chesterfields to each of the other three and made certain to light Francine's while Joseph flicked his own Zippo to light Abby's. The conversation picked up a bit; Jonathan and Joseph took turns telling the girls what they had missed in *Thunder Birds*, which was pretty much the whole movie and its hokey, unrealistic torn-between-two-would-be-lovers plot. They did enthrall the girls with an elongated tale of their brief encounter with Gene Tierney when she came back on base in July for some final shooting...an ensemble encounter that was actually shared by about two hundred other flying cadets one evening in the Officers' Club as she circulated among the would-be flyers and their instructors.

The boys had rendezvoused with both Francine and Abby at the streetcar stop in Polish Hill before taking the trolley downtown to the Senator earlier that evening. However, since Abby lived with her parents in the East Liberty section of the city, she and Joseph needed to take a different streetcar back than the one Jonathan and Francine would hop in order for Joseph to escort Abby home. This separation of the two couples worked out just fine for all of them.

Goodnights were said along with a "see ya later at home" exchange between Jonathan and Joseph as Abby's and Joseph's streetcar arrived first. Left alone again, Francine turned to Jonathan and said:

"Do you want to walk a bit before we go back? It's not too cold, I don't think."

Nearing 10:00 the temperature still hovered just around forty degrees, the same as the previous night when Jonathan and Joseph had walked back home from Dominic's after running into their buddy Joey DeMarco. The air was definitely chilly but even more than last night, Jonathan didn't feel it. He wrapped his left arm around Francine and pulled her close to him as they walked side by side, headed back towards downtown.

They walked in silence down Liberty Avenue towards the tip of downtown where the three rivers came together. There was the old blockhouse from Fort Pitt but that was beyond the warehouses and railroad yards; no place for the two of them at night. They cut back into the heart of downtown and walked aimlessly.

Francine had never told Jonathan exactly where that encounter with Donnie Yablonski had occurred – at the William Penn Hotel – but she was well aware as they walked around the downtown area that the red brick hotel was only a few blocks away most of the time they circled through the near-deserted streets.

She honestly didn't remember many of the details of what had happened given how drunk he had managed to get her, and as the months passed the memories of that night's details dulled even further until the whole sordid night might as well have only been a dream. Francine honestly thought that with the passage of a little bit more time it would be almost as if that night had never actually happened at all.

But could Jonathan ever come to see it that way? As a wispy, barely recalled aberration, so out of character from anything Francine had ever done before or would ever do again? No doubt Jonathan's mind had conjured up vile images of her and Donnie together as he imagined events that night as they may have happened. Could those invented images fade with time as well or – because they weren't the actual alcohol-tinged remembrances by one of the participants of what had indeed occurred – might they stubbornly and vividly persist for all time?

If only it hadn't happened! Francine felt a shudder run through her and in response Jonathan pulled her even closer to him as they walked. No doubt he thought that shivering was because of the chilly night, but Francine recognized it as a conveyance of the sorrowful regret that was washing over her now in waves. Even worse, she regretted that she was reliving segments of that night with Donnie even now as she walked along closely held by Jonathan. In the darkened movie theater, kissing Jonathan again and again, there had been not a single thought of that skunk Donnie Yablonski who had so callously taken advantage of her; why couldn't her mind have remained that way?

*   *   *

After exiting the streetcar at the stop on Negley Avenue in East Liberty, three blocks away from Abby's parents' house, Joseph and Abby walked in the opposite direction. Just as Jonathan and Francine were walking mostly wordlessly around downtown Pittsburgh during those same moments, Joseph and Abby sauntered along, holding hands and occasionally looking over at one another with sweet, sad smiles.

Joseph felt as if he had suddenly been thrust into the middle of some sappy love story movie; the kind where the star-crossed would-be lovers meet but, alas, the fates have dictated that they will never be together. He had been dragged to one or two of those during his senior year at Schenley by girls he had asked out; the implicit bargain had been that if Joseph would endure the silly mushiness on screen for an hour and a half, he would be rewarded with a little bit of necking afterwards. He had always thought those plots had been so contrived; deliberately written as such to appeal only to the sentiments of young girls who went to the movies, because who else could become enveloped in such foolishness? But now he was actually living one of those mawkish stories himself!

Ah, forget it, he told himself. He'd be gone in a couple days and Abby Sobol would go and find some 4-F guy at the War Production Board who would sweet-talk her and before you knew it, Joseph Coleman would be a distant memory to her. He already knew enough about her that she wasn't a flirty, one-guy-quickly-to-another kind of girl; for a short while at least his departure would leave a little bit of a hole in her. But for the meantime, he might as well enjoy this time with her; almost as if he met some gal out in Phoenix and then left her behind when he headed off to the war.

Joseph turned towards Abby and reached to turn her towards him. There, underneath the blacked-out streetlight on the deserted street, he began kissing her again. They remained in the kissing embrace for more than a minute and then Abby slid her head back, looking up at Joseph and smiling as she did.

"I better be getting home," she said softly.

"I know," Joseph replied but even as he spoke he was leaning in to begin kissing her again. She kissed him back for a few seconds then pulled back again.

"No, really; I better get home," she said again; a bit more insistently, but still sweetly.

Joseph sighed as he smiled at her. His arms dropped from the embrace and his left hand found her right one as they turned back in the direction where Abby's house was. They walked again in silence until they reached the stairs leading up to the elevated wooden front porch that looked almost identical to that at the Colemans' house.

"Would you like to go out again tomorrow night?" Joseph asked her as he walked her up the stairs.

"Uh-huh!" Abby replied enthusiastically. "I'd love to!"

"Okay," Joseph answered. "How 'bout I pick you up around 6:00?"

Abby thought for a moment.

"Better make that around 7:00. By the time I get home from work and have dinner, 7:00 would be a better time. Okay?"

"Okay," Joseph agreed as he leaned in again for the sweetest goodnight kiss he had ever experienced in his young life.

*   *   *

Jonathan was walking back home from Francine's house after seeing her to her door when he saw his brother about fifty yards away, walking homewards from the streetcar stop.

"Hey Joseph! Wait up!" he yelled at the top of his lungs. Joseph caught the sound of his brother's voice and turned around to see Jonathan trotting towards him, and paused to wait for his brother.

"So?" Jonathan said when he caught up with Joseph, only slightly out of breath.

Joseph just shrugged.

"Well?" Jonathan persisted. "How did it go?"

"I dunno," Joseph muttered. "Fine, I guess."

"What do you mean 'Fine, I guess?' What did you do after you left the coffee shop?"

Joseph shrugged again as the two of them slowly strolled along.

"Just took the streetcar to East Liberty and walked around for a little while; you know."

"So you gonna see her again?" Jonathan asked.

"Yeah, tomorrow night," Joseph replied morosely.

"So what's with the long face? You two hit it off just swell, right?" Jonathan asked, half-knowing the answer to his questions but asking them anyway.

"Yeah, that's just the problem. We hit it off; I see her tomorrow and them maybe if I can sneak away on

Thanksgiving a little bit then. And then that's it." Joseph's vow to himself of "oh well, just make the best of it" hadn't lasted very long.

"I don't know what to tell you," Jonathan answered sympathetically. "You never know, maybe she'll be the one you wind up marrying anyway, despite the war and everything."

"I suppose," Joseph replied. "Don't see how, but I suppose."

He looked over at Jonathan.

"So what about Francine?"

It was Jonathan's turn to shrug as they walked along.

"Same as you two, I guess," he replied. "We walked around downtown for a while and then I just took her home."

Joseph waited for more elaboration from his brother, but none was forthcoming.

"So what are you going to do?" he asked Jonathan after a few moments of silence.

Jonathan blew out a deep breath.

"I don't know," he answered, then looked at his brother.

"I guess we're both in more or less the same situation," he said to Joseph.

"Yeah," came the reply. "And it ain't a great one, either."

Just as they reached the bottom stairs leading up to their porch, Joseph spoke up after a few more moments of silence.

"That son of a bitch Tojo really messed things up for us with these girls, huh?"

Jonathan couldn't help bursting out into a hearty laugh at his brother's comment.

"Yeah, that bastard Hitler too," he added, to which Joseph joined in the ironic laughter.

They were still laughing when they walked through the front door, just as Gerald Coleman startled awake at the sound of the squeaking door. Benny Goodman was playing softly on the Philco.

"Hi Pop," the Coleman boys said in unison when they saw that their father was still downstairs and awake.

"Hi boys," Gerald replied. Seeing that they were still chuckling, he asked,

"What's so funny?"

"Ah nothing," Joseph replied. "We were just agreeing that Tojo and Hitler have no sense of romance, you know?"

It took Gerald a couple seconds to catch on to what Joseph meant.

"I suppose not," he replied in somber agreement. He looked over at Jonathan, who was taking off his flight jacket. Jonathan, sensing that his father was gazing at him, looked back at Gerald; locked eyes; and simply gave his father the thumbs-up sign; that "Ready; let's go!" signal that was quickly becoming popular among American flyers.

4 – Wednesday, November 25, 1942

Every person in the Coleman household over the age of sixteen bore the burden of a night filled with strange, disturbing dreams.

Gerald Coleman dreamed that he was sitting in his living room sometime a year or two later; maybe even farther into the future. The only other person in the room was Francine, who was either engaged to Jonathan or married to him – he wasn't sure which – and the two of them were listening to the radio; Jonathan was still away at war. Bob Hope was announcing the news, not doing his entertainment program, and they listened to him say: "Here's a United Press bulletin just in: FDR just announced that the war will go on for at least three more years; stay tuned for more details after this word from Pall Mall." In the dream Gerald and Francine looked at each other as Francine fiddled with the ring on her finger, seeming to want to remove it and not wear it any longer...

In Irene Coleman's dream she was walking back into the house following a trip to the grocery market and the bakery. Ruthie, a couple years older than she was now in real life, was sitting on the couch reading a copy of *Look*. "Look Ma," Ruthie said to Irene, "It says that Charlene got married to Clark Gable. Here's pictures and everything!" Irene set the bags of groceries down on the table so she could see what Ruthie was talking about, all the while wondering why Charlene had been too busy out in Hollywood to let her own mother know that she had gotten married.

Charlene Coleman's dream was set later that same day, during rehearsals at Allderdice. Instead of talking with Mrs.

Phillips about Charlene, Irene Coleman was embroiled in a furious argument with Judy Garland, who was standing on the auditorium's stage holding Toto from her Dorothy Gale role. Charlene kept hearing her mother utter the phrase "No daughter of mine..." over and over and over as she wagged her finger disapprovingly at Miss Garland, who finally tossed her head in despair and exited stage right – her little dog too – leaving Charlene Coleman and her talents behind forever.

Joseph's dream had him coming back from the war with an English bride. They were gathered at the first Thanksgiving after the war, whenever that might be, all of them seated around the Coleman table...including Abby Sobol, who kept sadly saying over and over again to Joseph in between bites of turkey and stuffing: "You told me to wait for you, and I did..."

Jonathan Coleman's dream began as a reprise of the one from the previous night, with Donnie Yablonski as his unwelcome best man as Jonathan and Francine became man and wife. In this one, though, in the midst of the dream Jonathan suddenly vanished and he watched omnisciently as the wedding ceremony continued with Donnie and Francine as the main participants, and Jonathan nowhere to be seen. And in the dream, Francine didn't seem the least bit fazed by the old switcheroo.

*   *   *

"Can I see that one over there in the back?"

Jonathan pointed towards a ring with what appeared to be a slightly smaller diamond than the one he had just handled before shuffling it back to the clerk at Boggs and

Buhl. The two had left the house around 9:30 that morning and arrived at the Savings Bank in Oakland, passbook in hand, right when the bank opened at 10:00. Jonathan withdrew the $200 he thought he would need and then they grabbed the streetcar into downtown and across the Allegheny to the North Side where the upscale department store was located.

Prices for rings had certainly gone up since last December! Jonathan still had the same $150 he had spent last year for Francine's engagement ring after he had returned the ring and gotten his money back. And since he had worked all winter and most of the spring before leaving for Thunderbird Field, he had made almost another $500, most of which he had saved. Still, he figured that the $200 he had brought with him should cover a ring just as nice as the one from last year; the rest of the money could stay put in the bank until after he came back from the war and they could use that money for their honeymoon. For superstitious reasons he had already decided that he was not going to buy her the same ring if it or one just like it were still in the case, given what had happened as he tried to give it to her and ask her to marry him before. But Jonathan had a fairly good idea of what he was looking for this time around.

But the prices! He had expected prices to be slightly higher because of the war, but that same ring from last year – at least he thought it was the same ring, or one very close to it – was now more than double the price! He asked the clerk if maybe the one he had just handed back might have had a better diamond than his from last year; maybe that was the reason for the higher price. But the clerk confirmed that not only was this ring equivalent in quality to what Jonathan described as the one he had purchased last year, that indeed prices had risen dramatically because of the war. Between both sides' insatiable need for diamonds for war materiel production purposes and the disruption of the flow of diamonds from Africa, prices were going to be sky high until after the war, the man explained.

"Do you think she'll like that one?" Joseph asked his brother.

Jonathan shrugged, then looked across the counter as the clerk was fishing for the next ring Jonathan had just pointed towards. Not that long ago, the man would be impatient with – perhaps even rude to – these two kids who obviously were shopping on the cheap. He would likely have moved on to another more prosperous customer after a dismissive "tell me when you see something I can help you with." Indeed, from a few days after Pearl Harbor through the first six months of 1942 the store's business in diamond engagement rings had boomed, and the clerk had made nearly twice as much money from commissions as he had in all of 1940 and most of 1941. Young men all around Pittsburgh were flocking to marry or become engaged to their sweethearts before leaving for the war, and almost every single one of them needed to buy a diamond engagement ring. But from the end of this past June, about the time the post-graduation weddings had all occurred, business at the ring counter had all but dried up. There had been a slight uptick in the past week or so with some of these soldiers back on Thanksgiving furlough, but no doubt this Christmas season would be far slower than last year's.

Jonathan examined the ring the man had handed him. He didn't know much at all about diamonds, but he had no doubt the one attached to this ring wasn't of particularly good quality. It was definitely smaller than the other one; *that* he knew for sure. Would Francine like it? She had only glanced at the original ring for a split second on Christmas Eve before quickly shutting the lid of the box, turning to Jonathan with tears in her eyes, and beginning to tell him…

Jonathan quickly shook away that unwelcome memory that had snuck up on him just like an enemy commando. He forced himself to concentrate on the ring in his hand, and the question he had begun to ponder: if Francine would like this somewhat understated engagement ring.

"Maybe we should go look at Gimbels or Joseph Horne," Joseph said rather undiplomatically, with the Boggs and Buhl sales clerk still standing right on the other side of the counter from them. Other department stores back in the heart of downtown would likely have lower-priced rings than this place a few blocks from the area on the North Side still called "millionaire's row" that had once been home to many of Pittsburgh's 19th century industrial barons.

The salesman, seeing the very real possibility of his sale evaporating, leaned forward conspiratorially towards Jonathan and, in a lowered voice, said: "I shouldn't do this, however…"

*   *   *

A middle-of-the-ground ring had been found with the magnificent savings of $50 knocked off the retail price of $250, allowing Jonathan to hand over every penny he had brought with him – except for four bucks for a bite of lunch and streetcar fare – and, in exchange, depart with an engagement ring for Francine. The boys decided to walk back into downtown across the bridge, killing a bit of time until they were ready to grab lunch. Given the magnitude of what Jonathan was planning to do that night, and given the consternation that ill-kept secret would of course cause in the Coleman house that afternoon, neither one wanted to stay around the house much that day. Tomorrow would be Thanksgiving and they would be there the entire day; by that time the deed would have already been done and Jonathan will have received his answer from Francine.

"What if she says no?" Joseph had asked him earlier that morning as they waited for the streetcar after leaving the Savings Bank. Jonathan had fully considered that possibility. Last night had been the sweetest of all possible reunions with Francine, and she had given every indication that if he could bring himself to pop the question she would accept. Still, an evening enraptured in the aura of this unexpected reuniting of the two was one thing; *really* putting everything that had happened behind them for all time, and then dealing with the inevitability of spending their entire engagement of two or three or more years apart from one another; well, that was quite another, much more ominous matter.

Jonathan's answer to his brother's question had been fatalistic.

"Well, if she does then I guess it was never meant to be. I'll come back after the war and if she's still not married then maybe we'll see where things stand; otherwise I'll just marry some other girl."

Thinking about his own dream from last night, Joseph asked:

"If she does say no, you think you might meet some girl over in England or France and wind up bringing her home?"

Jonathan shrugged.

"I suppose," he replied. "I don't want to talk about it, okay?"

"Yeah, okay," Joseph had replied, his thoughts half with his brother and half…well, on other matters.

Now, walking across the Sixth Street Bridge into downtown, Joseph asked his brother another question.

"Do you remember what the cheapest ring back there cost?"

Jonathan slowed his pace and looked over to his right at his brother.

"Joey," he said as he lightly shook his head, "don't even think about it."

For a split second Joseph thought about playing dumb in response to his brother's gentle rebuke, but figured that would be a waste of time.

"I'm just thinkin', you know? Maybe I get Abby a small engagement ring and then if I get back on furlough before shipping out, if things are still good I get her a bigger one…"

"Yeah, but how will you even know if things are still good?" Jonathan interrupted. "You'll be out at Thunderbird and then wherever else they send us after that, and she'll be back here. Other than writing letters back and forth every couple days, how will you know?"

Joseph lowered his head and slumped his shoulders.

"I dunno," he said morosely.

The two finished crossing the bridge in silence.

"You know, I don't know how," Jonathan said as they reached the downtown side just as the noontime sun broke through the last stubborn cloud mass still hanging on from the morning, "but I really think it will work out for you and her. I don't know exactly how, but I think it will."

"Yeah," Joseph replied with only a touch more of an upbeat tone.

*   *   *

"Now hear this! Now hear this! General Quarters! General Quarters! U-Boat warning! Now hear this! Now hear this…"

The *Augusta's* loudspeaker brought the ship to life, and sailors went scrambling to their battle stations. One of the other ships in Task Force 34 radioed that they had spotted a diving U-Boat off their starboard side and the entire Task Force immediately went to General Quarters.

Marty Walker shot out of his bunk and reached for his life jacket before rushing up to his radioman's post on the Captain's Bridge. Admiral Hewitt, the Task Force 34 commander, was talking to the ship's Captain as Marty slipped by the two and hurried over to his seat in front of the radio console that was occupied by one of the other radiomen.

"What's happening?" Marty said in a low voice to the other sailor.

"The *Ranger* spotted a U-Boat, maybe two of them," the sailor said, referring to the aircraft carrier traveling back to Bermuda with the rest of the task force. "They think maybe they also saw a periscope near the one they saw diving."

"They moving to attack?" Marty asked.

"Dunno," was the sailor's reply as he fiddled with a dial on the shortwave. "Would be a really great Thanksgiving present takin' a torpedo and winding up in the Atlantic after making it through all that back in North Africa though, huh?"

Marty shuddered at the words, at the very thought, but didn't reply as he relieved the other sailor at the radio and waited…and waited…

*   *   *

Rehearsals at Allderdice this day before Thanksgiving were set to begin earlier than a day earlier. Mrs. Phillips knew that nearly every single one of the girls in the show, and probably even a few of the boys, needed to get home and help their mothers as Thanksgiving preparations moved into high gear. The markets, bakeries, and butcher shops would all be closing by 5:00 this afternoon – many of them even earlier – and even more so than in previous years, there would be a rush of frantic last-minute food shopping this afternoon. Especially with so many either-or decisions mandated this year by ration stamps, nearly every mother across Pittsburgh expected today to be extra-stressful.

Irene had already gotten a jump on the shopping this morning, dragging Charlene out of the house with her shortly before 8:00 to visit the grocery market and then take the streetcar down to *J. Weisberg & Sons* for the final purchases of produce for tomorrow's feast. Given that mother and daughter were embroiled in the midst of this battle of wills over Charlene's performing aspirations, the morning spent together was surprisingly congenial; even cozily cheerful. Irene surprised Charlene into nearspeechlessness when, aboard the streetcar headed down to the Strip District and *Weisberg's*, she turned to her daughter and asked out of the blue:

"So what was this Mister Gene Kelly like when he spoke to you? A nice man?" She was thinking of the drawing on the movie poster of this Mister Kelly cheek to cheek with Judy Garland herself. Her own daughter had spoken to someone who was in a movie with Judy Garland!

It took Charlene close to ten seconds to gather her wits to respond to her mother's question.

"Um, yes; very nice," she finally stammered out. "He graduated from Peabody right before the Depression and Mrs. Phillips used to take tap dance lessons from him before he went to Broadway; he had a dance studio in Squirrel Hill."

Charlene proceeded to tell her mother what she knew of Gene Kelly's long slog to Broadway success and, more recently, his debut in that Judy Garland movie that would be at the Senator next week. Irene listened patiently to what her daughter said.

"So do you think you could stand to do what you said he did? Go to New York and get absolutely nowhere and then have to come back to Pittsburgh?"

Charlene's eyes narrowed at her mother's question, and Irene immediately added:

"I'm not saying that I approve or that I'm going to let you do this; I just want know how you would feel if you tried to do that and wound up coming back. Would you get it out of your system and then get ready to settle down?"

Charlene rolled her eyes in response her mother's follow-up. Even as she began her response she was surprised that she wasn't furious at what her mother had just said, but for whatever reason she wasn't.

"You just assume that I'm not good enough; is that it? You still think that the only future I have is as some boy's wife, and sooner than later. Right?"

Irene shrugged.

"I don't know anything at all about this show business, even though I know who Judy Garland is," she said quietly. "All I do know is that it's a hard life full of disappointment, just like I told you yesterday."

She looked away from Charlene, then back at her.

"Is it so wrong that I don't want my own daughter to go through disappointment and pain?"

Charlene sighed.

"No, Ma," she said as the streetcar slowed to a stop and the two of them prepared to exit for a quick trip to *Weisberg's* before heading back home and then to rehearsals at Allderdice.

"I guess it's not," Charlene continued. "But can't you stop to think for a moment that maybe that wouldn't be what happens?"

The controversy was tabled while the duo forced their way among the throngs also trying to get their hooks into their share of surprisingly robust piles of turnips, yams, and other fall vegetables at the produce market. Most of the shoppers figured that this Thanksgiving would be the final one in which these vegetables would miraculously appear in markets such as *Weisberg's*; by next year the war effort would be even more fully in swing and almost all the goods American farms would be able to produce would be headed overseas in the direction of the fighting soldiers and sailors, and it would be back to potato chips. So with the pleasant surprise of this bounty of lush produce for morning shoppers such as Irene and Charlene, ration stamps were gladly exchanged for the opportunity to surprise those at tomorrow's Thanksgiving tables.

Charlene and her mother barely had time to stop back home and drop off the produce before hopping back on a streetcar to take them to Squirrel Hill, where they walked the couple blocks over to Allderdice High. The arrived with only five minutes to spare before the rehearsal was scheduled to begin. Charlene spotted Mrs. Phillips, who looked back at the girl and noticed that her mother had indeed accompanied her this afternoon.

Charlene and Sammy were up third after Mrs. Phillips clapped the rehearsal to life. As Charlene watched the first two sets of performers, she let her mind wander to the words Gene Kelly himself had blurted out at her last Friday: "Little girl, I can see you have a great deal of talent; I really mean that." She was nervous; this performance in front of her mother was every bit as nerve-wracking, and had every bit as much at stake, as an audition in front of Busby Berkeley, Louis B. Mayer, and Irving Berlin all at the same time! Yet the more she thought about Mister Kelly's words, the more confidence she gained.

Then it was time. Charlene did what Mrs. Phillips so often urged her to do when the moment to perform had arrived: seek out that extremely fine line that lies between concentrating very, very hard on perfectly recalling words and notes and choreography and, on the other side of that line, letting herself go almost as if Charlene were simply standing back and watching herself perform rather than doing it herself. If you can find that line and stay right on top of it for your entire performance, Mrs. Phillips had told her time and again, you will do wonderfully!

By the time she and Sammy joined together to sing the final two lines of the song, Charlene knew with all the certainty in the world that this had been her best performance ever of *I Could Write a Book*; even better than the one last Friday. She snuck a glance at her mother, seated two rows behind Mrs. Phillips but still close enough for Charlene to read her face, and saw an astonished look on Irene Coleman's face. Charlene flashed a brief smile at her mother and carried it over to Mrs. Phillips as she exited the stage alongside Sammy Canter.

Ten minutes later it was time for Charlene's solo. She found that line of performance excellence once again and sang her heart out. This time after she finished she looked at Mrs. Phillips first and the woman seemed to actually have tears in her eyes! Charlene couldn't be positive since she was twenty or so yards away from where Mrs. Phillips was seated, but the director certainly seemed deeply moved by Charlene's performance.

The other performers went and by 1:45 Mrs. Phillips called a halt to the run-through, telling everyone how wonderfully they had performed this afternoon and that rehearsals would resume next Monday, exactly one week before the All-City High School War Bond Benefit. Everyone began to scatter as Charlene walked over to Mrs. Phillips just as Irene Coleman arrived at the same spot.

"Mrs. Phillips? I'm Charlene's mother. She said that you wanted to talk with me about this Mister Gene Kelly."

For a brief moment Mrs. Phillips was taken aback. She had told Charlene not to say anything to her mother about any conversations with Mrs. Phillips. Oh well, she thought to herself, it really doesn't matter, especially given that the conversation was about to go in a very different direction than Mrs. Phillips had envisioned only yesterday when she had spoken with Charlene.

"It's very nice to meet you, Mrs. Coleman," she said, shaking Irene's hand. "Your daughter is a lovely, very talented performer."

She paused to wait for Irene to acknowledge the complement; part of her strategy.

"I see she is," Irene agreed. "I don't know much about singing and dancing but I thought she did very well."

"Oh, she did more than 'very well,' " Mrs. Phillips replied very quickly. "She is by far the most talented performer of all of these high school boys and girls from all over the city."

Irene, feeling as if she were walking into a trap, didn't respond.

Might as well get right to the point, Mrs. Phillips told herself. She looked at Charlene, smiled, and then back towards Irene.

"Mrs. Coleman, Charlene no doubt told you that Mister Gene Kelly, one of our own from here in Pittsburgh, watched Charlene on Friday and couldn't stop talking about what a wonderful performer she is."

She paused for a second and then added, for effect:

"And Charlene didn't even perform as well as she did today; I think she was inspired because you were here to watch her."

No reaction from Irene Coleman. Mrs. Phillips thought to herself: what a tough cookie this woman is!

"Do you know who Dorothy Lamour is, by chance?" she asked Irene.

Irene just shook her head. In fact the name did sound familiar and Irene knew she had probably seen that actress in a film or two over the years, but at the moment she was in no mood to place these Hollywood people up on a pedestal as her daughter, and apparently Mrs. Phillips as well, did.

"She's a very famous actress and singer; she was in those two movies with Bob Hope and Bing Crosby, *Road to Singapore* and *Road to Zanzibar?*"

"I suppose," Irene replied noncommittally.

"You do know who Bob Hope and Bing Crosby are, though, don't you?" Mrs. Phillips asked. This time a flash of anger radiated from Irene's eyes.

"I don't live in a cave, Mrs. Phillips," she said coolly. "I know very well who they are."

"I'm sorry, I didn't mean to offend you. Charlene did say that you don't follow the movies much so I wasn't sure…"

"I listen to Mister Crosby on the *Kraft Music Hall* and my husband listens to Bob Hope all the time, and I know they're both in the pictures."

Mrs. Phillips just nodded; she wasn't going to get dragged into an off-topic argument with Charlene's mother.

"Well, Miss Lamour starred in both of those movies with Bob Hope and Bing Crosby, and they have another one coming out next year. She's a very big star, she's been in many other films, and she's the one who helped begin the War Bond tours so many of the stars have been doing since earlier this year."

At the phrase "War Bond tour" Irene's ears perked up but before she could interject Mrs. Phillips kept talking.

"She is beginning a short Bond tour in New York, Washington, and Philadelphia the day after Christmas and in her show she is going to have a group of high school-age girls performing popular show tunes, just like those Charlene sings so well."

Irene knew where this was going and she was already shaking her head, though Mrs. Phillips refused to pause.

"Mister Kelly apparently called someone at Metro Goldwyn who is working with someone from Paramount – that's where Miss Lamour has her contract – on the tour, and they would like Charlene to join the group..."

Irene was already adding a series of "No" retorts even as Mrs. Phillips continued, then interrupted the show director.

"Charlene told me that you wanted to try and convince me that she should be in shows here in Pittsburgh at the Playhouse..."

"That's what I had planned to discuss with you," Mrs. Phillips countered, determined not to let this woman get the upper hand and squash this chance of a lifetime for Charlene. "And I still believe that is a wonderful direction for Charlene after the New Year. But I just received the telephone call today from the man at Paramount..."

Irene began to glare at Charlene.

"Charlene didn't know anything about this," Mrs. Phillips shifted gears, coming to Charlene's defense. "This is as much of a surprise to her as it is to you; a very wonderful surprise!"

"You want me to have my daughter quit high school so she can…"

"That's not it at all," Mrs. Phillips countered again, feeling as if she were engaged in a verbal fencing match and that Charlene's mother was only hearing what she wanted to. "There is no need for her to quit school or even miss any school! There are only seven shows in total and they will all be completed by January 3rd, which is a Sunday. Three of the shows are in New York City and two each are in Philadelphia and Washington."

Sensing Irene about to interrupt again, Mrs. Phillips kept rolling.

"There are no high school boys in the show; only high school girls. There will be plenty of chaperones and the girls won't be out of the chaperones' sights for a single minute. And she will be back just in time to start school on January 4th."

With that, Mrs. Phillips paused. She had launched her salvo on Charlene's behalf, and she had done so with genuine enthusiasm. She had been surprised into shocked silence a few hours earlier when the Paramount production man called on behalf of Miss Lamour and said that Gene Kelly had placed a call to Metro Goldwyn over the weekend and recommended this certain girl – he didn't recall the girl's name, but she was doing the two numbers from *Pal Joey* in the Pittsburgh Pearl Harbor high school show – for this particular War Bond tour. Mrs. Phillips had presumed that Mister Kelly had been genuine last Friday in his praise of Charlene's talents to the girl and to Mrs. Phillips herself, but for him to have gone to the lengths to make a recommending phone call over the weekend? This was a major matter!

"Mrs. Phillips, thank you for your concern about Charlene. I will discuss the matter with her father but I don't believe we will want her to participate in a traveling War Bond show at the age of seventeen, while she's still in high school."

Mrs. Phillips sighed, looked at Charlene – the girl had a crushed look on her face and seemed about to burst into tears – and then back at the girl's mother.

"Mrs. Coleman, I understand how you feel about wanting to protect your daughter. I wouldn't even bring this up to you if I weren't convinced myself that she will be perfectly safe, not to mention that she has the talent to be very good in whatever they would want her to do. Remember also that the whole purpose of the tour is to sell War Bonds, and I know that both of her brothers are in the Air Corps, just like my own youngest son. His two older brothers are in the Army; both are in North Africa right now, so I have three of my own boys in uniform. These are very different times than any we've ever lived through, even during the Depression. I want my sons to have the best of everything while they are fighting, and I'm sure you do too. This isn't about Charlene wanting to go to Broadway or Hollywood, though maybe down the road a bit that will be in store for her. Right now this is about her doing a small part to help her own brothers and everyone else in uniform while they put their lives on the line, and unless she's going to become a nurse and join the WACs or WAVEs in a few years, this is what she can do for the war effort; and she can do this right now!"

As she spoke, Mrs. Phillips became more passionate; almost angry. She could certainly understand Irene Coleman's natural inclinations towards protecting and sheltering her daughter, but by God, didn't the woman realize that the world had so dramatically changed for all of them?

Irene was taken aback by the show director's near-sermon but wasn't about to let her, or Charlene, know that.

"I will discuss the matter with Charlene's father," she repeated.

"Come on, Charlene," she said, turning towards her daughter. "We need to make several stops on our way home before all the markets close."

Mrs. Phillips was certain that Charlene would burst into tears the moment she set foot outside of the high school, and her heart broke for the girl.

* * *

Several times on the way home; while at the markets; and then later while preparing dinner, Charlene tried to engage her mother in a conversation about this astounding news. Ordinarily, she would be on top of the world after learning that Gene Kelly himself had recommended she be included in a War Bond tour...and with Dorothy Lamour as the star attraction! *Everything* about this opportunity was absolutely perfect for Charlene: the proximity to home; the chance to spend several days in New York City, performing on stage at the famous Radio City Music Hall; and then still being able to get back home in time for school to start.

How could her mother be so cruel to flatly say no! She had told Mrs. Phillips that she would discuss the matter with Charlene's father, but Charlene knew how those "discussions" went: whatever Irene Coleman wanted, she and her iron will would get. How unfair it all was!

Irene, finally tired of her daughter's alternating sulking, fuming, and pleading, banished Charlene from her kitchen while she finished dinner. Charlene stomped upstairs and came as close to slamming her bedroom door as she would dare do in her mother's house.

A moment later she heard a light knock.

"What?" she snapped.

"It's Joseph," came the response.

"Sorry, come on in," Charlene replied back. The door opened and in came her brother.

"What's wrong with you?" he asked as he pulled out the wooden chair from her desk and grabbed a seat.

For several seconds Charlene glared at him in response to his choice of words but she quickly realized that he wasn't criticizing or mocking her; he really wanted to know. She told him an abbreviated version of the whole story, dating back to last Friday's rehearsals. When she finished, Joseph leaned back and just shook his head.

"Wow," he said. "You on stage with Dorothy Lamour! Would I love to see that!"

"Weren't you listening?" Charlene snapped at him. "I'm not going to *ever* be on stage with Dorothy Lamour, or anybody else, for you to see. *She* won't let me!"

"Ah, come on," Joseph replied. "You don't know that. You know how Ma is; she thinks we're all still kids. When she thinks about it, and when she talks to Pop, she'll come around; just watch."

Charlene looked at her brother disbelievingly.

"Are you serious?" she asked incredulously. "Once she makes up her mind she *never* changes it! She's always been that way!"

"Maybe," Joseph half-agreed, "but that's when we were all younger and that's before the war started. Everything is different now. Look at Jonathan and Francine. Earlier this year Ma probably would have strapped Francine onto a bomb and dropped her out of a B-24 right onto Hitler's head in Berlin if she could, but now after Jonathan proposes she'll have to get along with…"

"What?" Charlene interrupted. "Jonathan is going to propose to Francine?" This was news to her and Joseph suddenly realized that for all the talking that he and Jonathan, and for that matter Jonathan and their father, had done about the pros and cons of him getting back with Francine, no one had clued Charlene in. Charlene knew that Jonathan had gone out with Francine the previous night but apparently had no idea that the two of them had hit it off all over again and apparently decided to put the past behind them and turn the clock back, so to speak, to before last Christmas Eve.

Joseph gave his sister an abbreviated rundown of that particular situation and then wove in the sorrowful tale of Abby Sobol and himself.

"Oh no," Charlene said when Joseph had finished telling Charlene how unfair it all was that he had to leave just as he had met this wonderful girl. "How awful!"

"Yeah, well," Joseph said sullenly, "I suppose there's a chance that when I come back she'll still be here and won't have gotten married…"

Brother and sister sat there in glum silence, each dejected about their own predicaments but, at the same time, feeling for the other.

"At least Jonathan will be happy," Joseph finally said.

"I hope so," Charlene nodded, her lips pursed tightly.

*   *   *

Irene Coleman tried her best to create a festive spirit at her dinner table that Wednesday night. She directed questions at Ruthie and Thomas who, catching onto the sullen moods of the oldest three, tried to be as peppy as possible in their responses. Irene had resigned herself to the fact that indeed Jonathan was going to ask Francine to marry him this very evening, after all that had happened. He was twenty years old, after all, and a mother can't stop foolishness by a child that age as she had successfully done when Charlene had been sixteen with that Larry Moncheck nonsense.

Most important of all, Thanksgiving was tomorrow - almost certainly the final Thanksgiving all of them would spend together until after the war – and Irene was grimly determined that there was no way Charlene's sulking or Joseph's moping was going to ruin the holiday for the rest of the family. So starting right here and now, at Wednesday night's dinner table, Irene would take charge and do her best to foster the proper holiday spirit.

Beyond the war news from that afternoon's *Pittsburgh Press*, led by the promising news that the Russians had broken the Nazi siege of Stalingrad, the front page of the paper told of an impending penny and a half increase in the home delivery price of a quart of milk. Irene began grumbling at this news as Gerald related it to her until she realized that the two biggest drinkers of milk in the house – Jonathan and Joseph – hadn't been at home for months and would be gone again by the time the increase went into effect. Forced once again to confront the looming departure of her sons back to their Army Air Forces training, she abruptly halted her complaining.

Joseph departed quickly after dinner to pick up Abby at her parents' house and then make it back to Oakland where they were to see *Holiday Inn* at the Strand. At 6:15 the phone bell clanged in the Coleman household and Jonathan, closest to the phone in the living room since everyone else was still in the kitchen (except for Gerald, who had headed to his shoe shop for a short while to finish his work on the boys' baseball gloves), picked it up and answered.

"Hi Jonathan," came Francine's voice from the other end.

"Hi Francine," Jonathan replied nervously. Why was she calling here? He was supposed to be picking her up at her house in less than half an hour.

"Um, can I meet you at the streetcar stop?" Their plans for the evening called for Jonathan and Francine to see *The Black Swan*, the brand new Pirate movie with Tyrone Power and Maureen O'Hara that was just starting today downtown at the Fulton. Afterwards they would ride the incline up to Mount Washington to look down at the darkened downtown below them. Jonathan certainly would have preferred to pop the question to Francine as they gazed upon the magnificence of the downtown Pittsburgh lights as they were before the war, but the blackout of course made that impossible. They wouldn't be up there long anyway, given the late fall chill that would be magnified up on the mountain, but Jonathan wanted to ask for Francine's hand in a special place that the two of them would always remember...and certainly *not* in her living room where the terrible memories from last Christmas of handing her that ring still lingered in his mind.

"Why?" Jonathan asked. "I want to pick you up at your house. Aren't you home right now?" He wasn't going to formally ask Jack Donner for his daughter's hand before he asked Francine herself, but he realized that he hadn't seen Francine's parents for an entire year and it would be proper to at least renew acquaintances before he showed up there sometime tomorrow during their Thanksgiving celebration as Francine's brand new fiancé.

Francine hesitated. "I'm home, but I think it would be best if I met you at the stop."

"Why?" Jonathan asked again, sensing that something was definitely not right.

"Can we just meet there? Please?" Francine's tone was a combination of insistent and irritated at Jonathan's probing.

"Francine, what's going on?" Jonathan persisted. He didn't want to tell her anything along the lines of "I would like to say hello to your father" even though he was all but certain she knew The Question was forthcoming.

"Jonathan…" the pleading in her voice was worrisome.

Suddenly it occurred to Jonathan that the previous night when he had suggested that he and Joseph pick up Francine and Abby at Francine's house after work, given that Abby was eating dinner with Francine's family before their date, Francine had countered with "How about we meet you both at the streetcar stop instead? This way Abby won't be nervous with Joseph picking her up at my house." He hadn't thought anything of it at the time, but now he wondered…

He took a stab in the dark.

"Is there a problem with me picking you up while your parents are home?"

"Not my mother..." Francine muttered.

"Yeah, but what about your father?" An unsettling scenario was starting to form in Jonathan's mind.

No answer.

"Francine?" He was becoming irritated.

"Um," she finally stammered, "I don't think it's a good idea for my father to see you."

At first he waited for her to continue but finally had had enough.

"Francine, I'm coming over there right now."

"No!" came the instantaneous, panicky reply.

"Then you tell me right now what is going on!" Jonathan was aware that his own voice was raised and everyone else in the Coleman house could probably hear him; but right now he had bigger concerns.

"My father doesn't know about what happened last year," Francine said. "He thinks that you...um..."

It took Jonathan a moment to grasp what she was saying but before he could respond Francine continued.

"My mother knows all about it, but she told me not to tell my father; she didn't want him to think that I...well, you know..."

Jonathan couldn't believe what he was hearing.

"So let me get this straight," he said through clenched teeth, fighting to remain calm. Just then Thomas walked out of the kitchen into the living room. Jonathan cupped his hand over the phone's mouthpiece and said brusquely,

"Tommy, get outta here; this is private!"

Taken aback, the youngest brother's eyes widened as he hastily beat a retreat back to the safety of the kitchen. Thomas had no idea what had suddenly come over his older brother but he knew he wanted to be pretty far away from him at this moment.

Jonathan instantly felt badly about snapping at his brother, but apologies would have to wait.

"So let me get this straight," Jonathan repeated into the telephone, forcing himself to lower his voice. He spoke in terse, clipped tones. "Your father has thought this whole time that the reason we split up is because I did something to you like...like you did, and you've been afraid to tell him the truth because your mother told you not to say anything and you're just gonna go on with him thinking that *I* did something bad to *you* when it's the other way around. Were you *ever* planning on telling him?"

Jonathan heard a slight sob on the other end of the line but continued.

"That's just great, Francine," he said angrily. "If it were up to my Ma I wouldn't have anything to do with you after what you did, but I gave you another chance even though *you're* the one who got so stinking drunk as your excuse so you could let Donnie..."

A resounding clicking sound hit Jonathan's ear through the phone's receiver as Francine hung up on him.

Jonathan just stood there for a few seconds with the telephone handset pressed against his head, as if the connection might magically reoccur. Then he slowly placed the phone back onto the base, resisting the urge to slam the handset down so hard as to cause a clanging sound to resonate throughout the Coleman downstairs. He was angry with Francine, but he was also furious with himself, feeling much the same after those other angry, hateful words he threw at her that day back in February. And now here came the memories of last Christmas Eve all over again; the flashbacks washed over the floodgates he had erected to keep remembrances of that terrible night at bay. He walked slowly over to the coat closet, retrieved his A-2 jacket just as Thomas peeked into the doorway between the kitchen and the living room.

"Sorry 'bout yelling at you earlier, Tommy. I'm going out," Jonathan said and Thomas Coleman only nodded in response.

*   *   *

Marty Walker bolted awake in his bunk, his utility shirt drenched with sweat. In his dream – his nightmare – the U-Boat scare from earlier today hadn't turned out to be a false alarm, or just a might-have-been encounter in which the Nazi submarines were scared off by Task Force 34 bearing down on them. In the nightmare two U-Boats had launched torpedoes at the *Augusta* and scored direct hits. Sailors and officers abandoned ship, and Marty remembered going into the drink with O'Shannon – the kid he had talked to the previous night – along with, apparently, O'Shannon's brothers who in the dream were aboard the *Augusta* rather than serving in the Army and Air Corps, even though they were wearing their uniforms of the other services.

Also aboard the *Augusta*, and among the cluster of survivors who gathered together in the frigid North Atlantic waters, were Marty's cousins Jonathan and Joseph; Thomas was there also, and in fact so was his cousin

Charlene and even little Ruthie. Marty's sister Lorraine and his little brother Calvin were also floating with them, as were his parents and his Uncle Gerald and Aunt Irene.

In fact, everyone who should have been at a family Thanksgiving dinner back home was instead freezing in the icy ocean water in Marty's terrible dream, helplessly waiting to die.

Marty slid out of his bunk, removed his sweat-soaked utility shirt and fished in his tiny locker besides his bunk for another one, and then headed outside into the cool night without even stopping to enjoy a smoke. As reason and reality continued to strengthen their hold on his thoughts, Marty thought that the waters through which the ship was now sailing, not too far from Bermuda now, would likely not be nearly as cold as they had been in his dream. Still, he was well aware that the significant message of his dream was a very simple one: instead of being at home tomorrow with his parents and brother and sister and all the Colemans for Thanksgiving, he would instead be somewhere out in the ocean, closing in on a strange, distant port only a short time after being at war.

Marty thought back to those weeks after Pearl Harbor, when he had badgered his father to let him drop out of school so he could enlist. And then the three short months in which he buckled down especially hard, took extra classes, and graduated in mid-March ahead of the rest of his class so he could enlist immediately afterwards; then boarding the train for the Naval Training Base in Chicago on April 4th, one day before Easter. Back then a scenario such as this very one he was living at this moment — standing alone outside under the stars on the deck of a Navy cruiser after participating in the largest amphibious assault the world had ever seen — seemed so grown up; almost romantic, in a manly way. Now, he only wished that he were on his way back home to be with his family and that he could put the whole damn war behind him forever instead of wondering what sea battle or invasion awaited the *Augusta* next…and if in that next one he and his crewmates wouldn't be so fortunate when it came to the outcome.

He thought, at least for the moment, that he did not want to sleep any more this entire night until daylight came and the ship would hopefully be in sight of Bermuda as Thanksgiving Day of 1942 arrived.

* * *

During the streetcar ride downtown Jonathan tried his best to think about the ticket booth girl at the Senator and force any and all thoughts of Francine from his mind the instant his conscience tried to force him to think about her. He kept recalling the ticket girl's flirty words: "Back again? You must *really* like this movie!" Would she say the same thing when he sauntered up to the ticket booth tonight? Would she remark on the fact that last night he had been there with a girl but tonight was apparently dateless? Would she then invitingly say something along the lines of "I'm done at 9:30; wanna stick around until I'm free?" The exact words didn't matter, Jonathan thought to himself as the streetcar bell clanged with the trolley approaching the stop near Penn Station; one more stop to go.

A moment before the streetcar operator was ready to shut the doors and pull away from the stop, Jonathan suddenly jumped out of his seat and hopped off the car. He felt like walking the last quarter mile. He forced away the memory of walking around downtown the previous night, his arm wrapped tightly around Francine half the time or holding hands with her the rest; apparently last night had just been a brief journey backwards in a time machine, and now Jonathan was back in the present.

Jonathan certainly had previously had very different plans for this next-to-last evening at home during his furlough, but just like his instructor out at Thunderbird Field kept telling him: "A good pilot reacts quickly and accordingly when the unanticipated occurs." And *that* was exactly what Jonathan was doing, he reasoned to himself: reacting quickly and accordingly; nothing more.

*   *   *

Gerald Coleman returned home around 8:15 and immediately sensed the terrible tension hanging over the house; even worse than it had been earlier in the evening during dinner. He knew something was amiss that involved Charlene, but earlier when he had asked his wife what was going on she tersely said "We will discuss it later." Gerald just let the matter drop, figuring that it would either resolve itself or Irene would eventually consult with her husband about whatever the problem was.

Now, though, Thomas was sitting sullenly listening to *The Adventures of the Thin Man.* As soon as he realized his father had entered the living room, he looked at Gerald and said:

"Something happened with Jonathan and Francine."

Thomas told his father the little bit that he knew – including that Jonathan had snapped at him while he had been on the phone arguing with Francine – but he had precious few details to offer to clue his father in to what had happened. After learning that Jonathan had left on his own, Gerald had a flashback to last Christmas Eve much as Jonathan had gone through a little while earlier. Realizing that there was no way to track his son's location to find out where he had gone, Gerald did the only thing he could do: he sat down with Thomas to listen to the rest of the *Thin Man* and wait for Tommy Dorsey's program that was up next.

Before the bandleader's program came on, though, Irene Coleman appeared in the doorway to the living room. Gerald saw her and instantly knew that she wanted to discuss Charlene. He got up from his easy chair, patted Thomas on the shoulder as he walked by, and followed Irene into the kitchen.

Irene walked over to the stove and poured a cup of fresh coffee for her husband as well as one for herself, and the two of them creaked into the hard-backed wooden kitchen chairs. Gerald had already lit a Pall Mall when he came into the house and it was time for another, but when he offered one to Irene she waved off the cigarette. This *was* serious, Gerald thought to himself, if his wife was too upset to smoke.

Irene related the entire tale of Charlene, Mister Gene Kelly of Broadway and Hollywood, Mrs. Phillips, the Pittsburgh Playhouse, and this afternoon's bombshell news of some Hollywood men wanting Charlene to participate in a War Bond tour with that actress who was in the movies with Bing Crosby and Bob Hope. Even as she was relating one part of the saga after another, Gerald could tell that his wife was slanting the story to make it all seem like so much girlish foolishness, not to mention a terribly unbecoming proposition for a young high school girl.

When she had finished, Gerald leaned back, lit another cigarette as he got up to pour himself another cup of coffee, and looked at Irene.

"If she went to New York and those other cities, the movie people would pay for everything, right?"

That very question caused Irene to sit upright in her chair.

"What do you mean?" she challenged. "What does that matter?"

Gerald answered his wife's question by not actually answering it, waiting for her to pick up on his wordless response.

"You're not actually thinking about letting her go on this War Bond tour, are you? What nonsense!"

"Is it?" Gerald replied, as soothingly as he could. "If she's as good as everyone says she is, maybe she should have the opportunity to do something like this while she can."

Irene's eyes were wide open with disbelief.

"She's just a young girl! She has no business going to places like New York City and Philadelphia with some movie star. You know what happens with those people!"

Gerald's eyes narrowed.

"I don't think they would leave her alone to run around New York by herself or with other high school girls and get in trouble, do you? Won't they have chaperones for them?"

Irene had "conveniently" forgotten to relate the chaperoning details to Gerald that Mrs. Phillips had described to her earlier this afternoon, but now she was forced to add those particulars to the story.

"Why not let her get this out of her system while she's young," Gerald offered after Irene related what Mrs. Phillips had told her about the chaperones, "and this way when she meets her husband in a year or two she'll be ready to settle down? Especially if she's good she will have wonderful memories to tell her children about."

Gerald paused for a moment and then continued.

"Besides, with everything around us so different now…"

"Stop saying that!" Irene nearly screamed as she interrupted. "I'm tired of hearing everyone say that! Charlene keeps saying that everything is different, and that Mrs. Phillips said that, and you were telling Jonathan that…"

So she was eavesdropping on Jonathan and me the other morning, Gerald thought to himself.

"I don't want to keep hearing everyone say that everything is different because of the war!" Irene continued, fury radiating from her eyes.

"But it is," Gerald said kindly; sadly. "Everything changed with Pearl Harbor. This war is so different than the Great War was. Back then life here at home was interrupted and everyone pitched in for the war, but that was nothing like what we've already seen this time. And it's only going to keep changing even more…"

"Stop saying that!" Irene repeated, but this time her voice weakened and tears began to form in her eyes. "I don't want things to be different, I just want my children. Jonathan and Joseph are going away again in two days and we don't know when we'll see them again. I do *not* want Charlene to go away!" With her utterance of "not" Irene pounded her fist on the kitchen table, causing both coffee cups to rattle and nearly topple from the small shock wave.

"Irene," Gerald said soothingly, using his wife's name which he rarely did, "I know. But from everything you said Charlene will only be gone for a very short while, they'll take very good care of her, and then she'll be back home right before school starts. And then that will be that."

"No it won't," Irene Coleman began sputtering as a couple of tears streamed down her cheek. "She'll be back for school alright but then she will start going on more Bond tours after she graduates, and then she *will* go to New York or all the way out to Hollywood…"

Gerald didn't quite understand what his wife was saying, and said so.

"Because she *is* very good," Irene said quietly, still lightly sobbing. "I watched her this afternoon and I don't know much about singing and dancing but everyone says she is the best one out of everybody in the show and they're right. I thought this Gene Kelly was just some Hollywood huckster who just happened to be from Pittsburgh, and that he had underhanded intentions towards Charlene; but he really did think that she's good enough to be on Broadway or in the movies."

Gerald finally seemed to be catching on to what was really bothering his wife.

"So you're worried that Charlene will leave us in a couple of months after she graduates and that she *will* be successful and then stay in New York or Hollywood?"

"I guess," Irene said reluctantly, for the first time coming to grips with what apparently was really bothering her so much. "I still think she will be in for terrible disappointment because no matter how good she is, there will be other girls who will do…things to get parts. And God forbid that Charlene ever gets those ideas in her head!"

Gerald was shaking his head as his wife put words to those distasteful, unthinkable thoughts.

"Why don't we let her go to this War Bond tour?" Gerald sensed his opening. "She will be doing good things for soldiers like Jonathan and Joseph and everyone else; that's the most important thing of all."

"*Speaking* of Jonathan," Irene shifted the topic of conversation, sensing she was on the ropes about Charlene and wanting to avoid any final consent on her part, "I suppose Francine broke his heart again, just like I *knew* she would." Sorrowful sobbing had suddenly given way to vindictive bitterness in her tones.

"We don't know what happened," Gerald countered. "Thomas told me that Jonathan left after he was arguing with Francine on the telephone, but we don't know what it was about. Maybe they'll work it out."

"I don't *want* them to work anything out," Irene hissed. "She did a terrible thing last year and I knew that when Jonathan started sniffing around her again she would do something bad again."

"Irene," Gerald said, tight-lipped, "we don't know that at all. I think it's probably some sort of misunderstanding left over from last year that they haven't worked out yet. Remember he's only been home a few days and he hadn't seen her in months. All it took was one date and he's crazy about her again, enough to ask her to marry him…"

"Maybe she said 'no' again," Irene interrupted. "Maybe she led him along when she saw him at lunch in Oakland and then last night, and now she got what she wanted with him wrapped around her finger and *then* she told him she wouldn't marry him."

A deep sigh escaped from Gerald Coleman.

"I don't think you'll ever like Francine; is that it?" he asked.

"How could I after what she did?"

"But suppose the two of them can put all of that behind them; you know, wartime foolishness…"

Irene was just about to explode at Gerald but he held up his hand in that "stop" motion.

"Regardless of whether you like it or not, or whether you want to admit it or not, people are doing strange things." He repeated much of what he had offered to Jonathan the other morning, knowing that Irene had eavesdropped on at least some of that so this wasn't exactly fresh news.

"And you know what's the most important thing of all?" he added.

"What?" Irene asked.

"Well, back in the Great War when I went over to France, even though I hadn't yet begun courting you I already knew that I wanted to marry you."

He reached across the kitchen table and laid his large cobbler's hand on top of Irene's; a tender, albeit infrequent, gesture of affection from husband to wife.

"Even though I had a fairly easy time during the war, I still thought that at any time I could wind up getting thrown in the trenches. I kept thinking about you back here at home and that kept me going the whole time I was there; the idea that if I made it through the war I would come home and there you would be."

He shook his head sadly; something he had been doing a great many times the past few days.

"This war is going to be terrible for both of our boys," he said in lowered tones in case Thomas was outside with his ear pressed against the kitchen door. "I hope and pray that they make it through and still they will see and go through things that will affect them the rest of their lives. I really believe that they each need to have a girl back here to think about all the time, to think about coming home to, and that will help get them through some tough jams. Both of them, too; not just Jonathan with Francine, but also Joseph and this new girl Abby. It doesn't matter that he just met her, and maybe when he comes back they will figure out they're not right for each other. But at least while he's over there he will have a girl back home, same as his brother."

Sensing the question that Irene was about to ask, Gerald continued.

"And I'm not saying Joseph should get engaged to this girl; not after only two days. She should just be that girl waiting for him back home, like in the movies."

Irene let out a combined sigh and sob as she lowered her gaze to the kitchen table for a moment then looked back at her husband.

"If things have changed this much, do you think they will ever get back to the way they were before the war?" she asked her husband.

"I don't know; I hope so," was his reply as he rose from the table. He rested a hand on his wife's shoulder for a moment, the same gesture he had done to Thomas a little while earlier, before he walked over to the kitchen door and opened it. Thomas was sitting across the room next to the Philco, listening to Tommy Dorsey.

"Go get your sister," Gerald said to his son before he turned back into the kitchen.

"About Charlene..." he said to his wife as he walked over to the stove for another cup of coffee. He had a feeling this would be a long night, so hopefully Irene would put another pot of coffee on the stove soon.

*   *   *

"You won't believe it! I'm going to go on a War Bond tour with Dorothy Lamour!" was the thrilling news that Charlene Coleman absolutely, positively had to share with her cousin Lorraine over the telephone that very night. News this wonderful just could not wait until the cousins saw each other tomorrow on Thanksgiving Day.

5 – Thursday, November 26, 1942

Jonathan Coleman saw that the living room lights were still lit, even though it was now a few minutes past 12:30 A.M. For a brief second he thought about not stepping on that first stair on the way up to the front porch and, instead, finding a bar that was still open. He just wasn't in the mood for conversation with anyone – his father, Joseph, and certainly not his mother – right now. The questions – "What in the world happened with you and Francine?" or "Where have you been all night?" or "What about the engagement?" – were ones he had no desire to field at this hour…or at all, for that matter.

The problem was that now that it was Thanksgiving Day, at least by the clock having ticked past midnight, no bars remained open…at least none that Jonathan knew of. In fact most had closed by 10:00 Wednesday night as even the barkeeps wanted to head to their homes before the holiday the next day. No coffee shops or diners were open because of the holiday, so late-night coffee and pie was every bit as elusive as an Iron City or Duquesne at the moment.

Sighing, Jonathan began to climb the steps up to the porch; might as well get it over with, he thought to himself. He turned the doorknob and walked inside and saw, as expected, his father waiting up for him. Joseph was there also. Both were listening to the Philco which had its volume turned down low. Jonathan couldn't catch what was playing; one of the Dorseys, he thought, but he wasn't certain.

"Are you alright?" was the first thing Gerald Coleman asked his son after Jonathan shut the front door.

"Yeah," Jonathan replied in a subdued voice.

"Go get some coffee," Gerald said, nodding to the kitchen. Implicit in what he said, even without having to add the words, was "and then come back in here and sit down so we can talk."

Jonathan complied. The coffee pot was about three-fourths full but he had a hunch this was at least the second or third go-around of the night for the old coffee pot. He wondered how long Joseph had been sitting here; after all he had been out with Abby tonight. He wanted to ask Joseph how his date had gone and how he was feeling about Abby right now, but he knew that his father wouldn't hear of any discussion at the moment other than Jonathan's disappearing act.

He walked back into the kitchen and plopped down on the sofa. He was dog-tired and wanted to get this over with so he could get some shut-eye.

"Where did you go?" Gerald asked when he saw Jonathan settled.

"I was downtown," Jonathan replied.

"Where downtown?" His father, apparently, had adopted the Irene Coleman school of interrogation for this particular conversation.

"Just around," Jonathan replied, hoping that his father would just move on to his next question.

"For five or six hours? What were you doing?"

Jonathan sipped his coffee.

"I went to see that pirate movie by myself," he replied, looking over at Joseph as he answered. "That one with Tyrone Power and Maureen O'Sullivan that I was going to take Francine to."

"You were gone a lot longer than that," Gerald challenged.

Jonathan shrugged.

"I saw it twice then walked around for a while, then went to get some coffee, then walked around some more."

He began to get agitated.

"I *am* twenty years old and almost an Army Air Forces lieutenant, you know," he said to his father with his eyes narrowed. "I *can* go watch a movie and then go sit in a diner if I want."

"Yes, I know you are," his father replied without reacting to the irritation in Jonathan's voice. "We were worried about you, that's all."

Gerald drew a deep breath.

"You want to tell me what happened with the phone call with Francine?"

"Not really," came the reply.

"Tell me," Gerald wasn't giving his son any quarter.

"Geez, you're starting to sound like Ma," Jonathan snapped at his father. "Leave me alone, alright?"

Joseph's eyes widened at the tone his brother was using with his father, and fully expected his father to respond in kind. Instead Gerald refused to take the bait.

"Fine," Gerald Coleman responded. "What I know is that you and her had some sort of fight over the phone and you stormed out of here and disappeared for half the night. What I also know is that your mother has been worried sick about you."

Jonathan was about to interrupt with another chorus of "I'm twenty years old and almost a lieutenant" but his father held up his hand to silence his son.

"And I was worried about you also," Gerald continued. "I know that you" – he then looked over at Joseph – "and you will both be over at the war soon, and that while you're out in Arizona you boys go out sometimes. You're men now. But I'm worried that you lost your temper yet again over something with Francine, and it's when you're not thinking clearly that you wind up doing things without thinking them through. And pretty soon you can't afford to do that."

"What do you mean 'yet again?' " Jonathan challenged.

His father's lips coiled into a tight smile, but by no means a warm one.

"Don't you remember last Christmas Eve? When you punched your brother in the nose? And then even after you said you wouldn't, you were going to go beat up Donnie? And all that was *after* you got in the fight down at the recruiting station when you were drunk. *That's* what I mean by doing things without thinking them through…yet again."

"I didn't do anything like that," Jonathan answered defensively. "I mean tonight. I didn't even have a single beer, and I certainly didn't get in any fights."

"Yes, but you stormed out of here without a word to anybody and you did that immediately after whatever it was that you got into a fight with Francine about. You still lost your temper; maybe not as bad as last time, but you still did."

Gerald sat forward, looked at Jonathan and then Joseph, and then back at Jonathan.

"Look," he said, "I'm going tell both you boys this again because you need to hear it. Do you both remember what I told you last Christmas after your fight, when I marched you boys down to the shop to get to the bottom of what had happened? That if you lost your cool over in the war you very likely will wind up getting killed?"

A muttered "yeah" came from each of Gerald's sons.

"And do you" – he looked squarely at Jonathan – "remember what I told you about needing to save up the fight in you for when you really need it, when maybe you're in the middle of a battle or up in the air and you need to call on it at just the right time?"

Jonathan started to protest.

"I said that I didn't get into any fights…"

Another "stop" hand motion from Gerald.

"Yes you did," Gerald countered. "Maybe it wasn't a fist fight with your brother or anybody else but you did get into a fight with Francine over the phone, and you were on your way to ask her to marry you. Now how in the world could you suddenly go from wanting to marry her to not only fighting with her but then wandering all over the city or whatever it was that you did?"

"It's what she said," Jonathan offered in response to his father's accusation.

Gerald let out a small chuckle.

"If I stormed out of this house and went to a movie by myself every time your mother said something that made me mad, you boys would have seen me a lot less when you were growing up. You just can't do that, Jonathan. You just have to let some of those things roll off your back, cool down, and then forget about it; just like I was saying."

He leaned back for a brief moment then forward again, lowering his voice.

"Tell me what she said that made you so mad." This time the words were a command that could not be denied, much like one issued by one of the boys' flying instructors out at Thunderbird Field.

Jonathan related a jumbled version of what had transpired with Francine on the telephone.

"What she did was wrong," Gerald said flatly when Jonathan had finished speaking. "Whether or not she told her father what happened with Donnie is a private thing, but she should not have gone on letting him think *you* had done something bad to her."

Jonathan's face immediately took on a look of self-satisfied vindication at his father's words, but that look immediately vanished when Gerald continued with:

"But *you* were *more* wrong," he said accusingly, but not unkindly. "Something like that you can get past, but instead you let it get to you and before you know it you hung up the phone on her and walked out of..."

"She's the one who hung up on me," Jonathan interrupted in protest.

Gerald shrugged.

"It doesn't matter," he retorted. "You still walked out and went downtown, instead of walking right around the corner to her house and straightening everything out. It's far more important for the two of you to make things right than to worry about her father. That's for her to work out eventually."

"And in the meantime he hates me because he thinks I did something I didn't?" Jonathan challenged. "That's not right!"

"So you think having your girl's father not like you is the end of the world? Your grandfather – your Ma's father – never liked me but that didn't stop me from courting your Ma and asking her to marry me."

"Grandpa didn't like you?" Joseph interjected. He had no memories of Irene's father at all given that Dawid Walker had passed away when Joseph was only three years old. There had been very little conversation about the man in the Coleman house over the years, though pictures of Irene's father were still scattered on the hallway walls and end tables in the house.

"No, not at all," Gerald replied, knowing that he had never before trekked down this path with his sons. He proceeded to tell Jonathan and Joseph how despite Irene's mother conspiring with Gerald's own mother as far back as 1912 to match Gerald and Irene, Dawid Walker had felt that Gerald, a mere cobbler's apprentice, occupied a station in life beneath what his daughter should be entitled to in a husband. For a simple immigrant, Irene's father had been a man of not only lofty aspirations but he conveyed a pretentious, self-important demeanor even though his own profession was that of a simple shopkeeper. In fact, Gerald often thought, Irene's brother Stan was very much like their father had been; that was largely the reason why Stan had gone crazy in the stock market during the '20s with money he should have tucked away for his family's future instead of getting wiped out in the Crash.

"I'm saying that you should just forget all about that and let him be," Gerald continued. "When you give him a grandson or two, or even a pretty little granddaughter, he will have long forgotten about what he thought you did. He'll see his daughter happy and a mother and realize that you're not a bad guy after all. And even if he doesn't, Francine knows that you didn't do anything to her; that's more important than anything."

Jonathan sat back as he absorbed his father's words. He had been so certain he had been in the right. But as he listened to his father he was now certain that he had badly overreacted to what Francine had reluctantly admitted over the phone. His Pop was right: it barely mattered that Jack Donner thought Jonathan had done something he hadn't, especially when time with Francine was so preciously short as his furlough ticked away!

Gerald could tell by the look on Jonathan's face, by the way he began to slump on the sofa, that he had gotten through to his boy.

"Go see her first thing tomorrow morning," he said. "Make it right; she'll forgive you."

"I'm not so sure," Jonathan said.

"She will," Joseph interjected. "She came and found Abby and me at the Strand and told us about the fight. She was crying; you know, *really* upset. But she kept saying over and over that it was all her fault, that she had messed things up. Abby wound up going home with her; we didn't even get to see the rest of the movie."

Joseph had a forlorn look on his face, and Jonathan suddenly felt very badly about having at least partially caused Joseph's final date with Abby Sobol to end prematurely.

"Sorry," Jonathan muttered to his brother, who just shrugged in response.

"I guess I'll go see her tomorrow morning and apologize," Jonathan continued as he looked back at his father.

"Good," Gerald nodded, and then added:

"And you know what else, right?"

For a few moments Jonathan was puzzled, not following what his father was getting at. But eventually he realized that his left hand was in his pants pocket fiddling with the Morgan dollar; he hadn't even realized he was doing it. His brain went to work, lightning fast, trying to recall if at any other time earlier this evening he had been doing the same thing, but was fairly certain he hadn't.

He withdrew the silver coin and held it up to his father.

"You mean this?"

Gerald was nodding even before Jonathan finished his short question.

"You didn't hold onto it earlier at all tonight, especially when you were on the phone, did you? To help you keep your cool?" father asked son.

"No," Jonathan replied, shaking his head. He looked at the coin in his hand, taking note as he almost always did of the significant wear that was no doubt largely due to his father having held or rubbed the coin repeatedly over the years, and then back at his father.

"You really think this would have made a difference?" he asked his father skeptically.

Gerald shrugged.

"I think it would have if *you* thought it would have," he replied.

Jonathan nodded and thought back to last Christmas and his father's words as Gerald handed his son that talisman: "I think you need this now, and I want you to have it."

"Yeah, I guess so, Pop," he said.

Gerald rose from his chair.

"You boys go on up and get some sleep. I'm going to have one more cup of coffee then turn in."

"Aren't you tired?" Jonathan asked, eyeing the grandfather clock that showed it was now past 1:00 in the morning.

"I am," Gerald acknowledged, "but it's been a long day and I want to sit for a little while and just listen to the radio."

*   *   *

His sons had departed for the upstairs floor in the house by the time he returned to the living room. Gerald eased himself back into his chair and turned the Philco's volume up just a touch; not too high so he couldn't think, but loudly enough to catch Jimmy Dorsey's orchestra and *Tangerine*.

He chuckled to himself; a melancholy, bittersweet chuckle. After the shock of Pearl Harbor had worn off and then before Jonathan and Joseph left for Arizona six months later, Gerald tried to take the entire family to the movies at least once each week despite being so very, very tired from working at the war plant as well as keeping his little cobbler business going. One of the movies they had seen back in February was *The Fleet's In*, one he had especially picked out to see because Jimmy Dorsey and his orchestra were featured in the movie...and in fact this very song, *Tangerine*, had been introduced in that film and had quickly become a smash hit on the radio.

One of the stars of that movie was Dorothy Lamour...one of Gerald's favorites from her couple of zany films with Bob Hope and Bing Crosby. And now, after coming to an understanding with Irene, their little girl would soon be going on a short War Bond tour with that very same Dorothy Lamour!

It's all moving far too fast, Gerald thought to himself as he sipped his coffee. Just like Irene, he was saddened by the overwhelming disruption that had been brutally thrust on all of their lives since Pearl Harbor and what it all meant to their family. Unlike Irene though, Gerald seemed more willing to accept the inevitability of that upheaval and to try and adjust to it as best he could, whereas his wife seemed to want to fight to the bitter end to keep the change at bay for a little bit longer.

He thought about tonight's events. Quite possibly all would be well with Jonathan and Francine, and Gerald allowed himself a small touch of self-gratitude that if indeed that would be the case, he had played a role in helping his oldest boy with this particular problem.

But Gerald couldn't help think that Jonathan – Joseph also – *needed* his advice for at least a while longer, but because of the war they were going away and wouldn't be around for their father to help them. Gerald was dismayed – and more than a little bit worried – that this very night might well be the final time he would ever be able to offer important, fatherly advice to his boys when they needed it. Presuming they came back from the war safely, Jonathan would be twenty-two or twenty-three, or maybe even older, and Joseph would also be a fair bit over twenty years old. Each will have become a man not only because of the number of years of life he will have clocked by then, but even more so by what they will have seen, done, and survived during the war.

Gerald hoped – he prayed – that everything he had been able to say to and do for his sons to this point will have been enough. He felt as if he had been forced to compress the final few years of fatherly advice he might have dispensed to Jonathan and Joseph into a mere handful of days. He so much wished that they all had more time for him to keep at least a little bit of an eye out for them, but he sadly acknowledged that it wasn't to be.

*   *   *

"Was she really crying?" Jonathan asked his brother in hushed tones as they were climbing the stairs.

Joseph blew out a breath.

"I'll say," he said, also in a lowered voice. When they reached the top of the stairs he nodded to Jonathan to follow him into his own room, which was the farthest away from where their mother might be able to hear them talking if she was still awake.

"We could barely understand what she was saying," Joseph continued after shutting the door to his bedroom. "She was blubbering something about having a fight on the phone with you, and then something about her father, and who knows what. People around us were getting mad so we got up and went out to the lobby with her."

Joseph plopped himself down on his bed.

"She said something about you going down to the Senator to make time with that ticket window girl and at first I thought she said that's what you did or maybe yelled at her over the phone that you were going to do, but then I figured out that she was saying instead that *maybe* you…"

Joseph halted as he saw the guilty look appear on Jonathan's face. His eyes widened and his mouth dropped open.

"Oh, you didn't!" he said to his brother.

Jonathan recovered from the surprise of his brother's words and shook his head.

"Nah…"

But before he could say anything else Joseph interrupted.

"Come on, I saw the look on your face!"

Jonathan looked away, then sighed and looked back at his brother.

"I'll tell you something but you have to swear to keep it a secret, especially from Abby. Okay?"

Joseph Coleman honestly wasn't sure he wanted to hear what he thought his brother was about to say, but he nodded and said, "Okay."

Jonathan sighed again as he leaned up against the bedroom wall next to his brother's bed.

"I *was* going to, and in fact took a streetcar down to the Senator. I figured that if things were over with Francine because of her father, then why not, you know? I jumped off at Penn Station and was walking there, but when I got about fifty yards away I just crossed the street all of a sudden and kept walking. I didn't even look over to see if that girl was there."

He paused for a moment to gather his thoughts before continuing.

"This is going to sound strange, but it was almost as if some giant invisible hand grabbed me and started pushing me across the street. I kept thinking that I wanted to go make time with that girl, you know, she was flirting with me last night so I figured if she was there things might get interesting, right? But all the while I'm thinking this I swear it was like looking down and seeing my feet heading across the street even though I wasn't telling them to; like I wasn't even in control. You know what I mean? It sounds crazy when I say it to you, but I swear that's what it felt like."

"Wow," Joseph said. He thought about what his brother had told him. Only a couple days ago he would have hoped that Jonathan would have headed straight for the Senator, made time with the ticket girl, maybe taken her inside to the balcony and had a good old time with her in the dark…anything to get back at Francine for what she had done with Donnie. Now, though, after seeing the two of them together the previous night, and after experiencing what he was feeling about Abby, he was extremely glad to hear his brother say that not only had nothing happened with that other girl but at the last moment he chickened out from even making a play for her.

"So what did you wind up doing? Where were you for so long?"

"Just what I said downstairs. I went to see that Tyrone Power picture by myself and stayed through it twice. I kept hoping Francine would show up there; you know, come to find me…"

Joseph laughed.

"Abby suggested that to her," he interrupted. "Right when Francine was saying that you probably were making a play for the ticket girl. She said that you were probably down at the Fulton all by yourself and that Francine should go down there to find you, and that we would go with her. But you know what Francine said?"

"What?"

"She was going home because she was sure you would show up there despite what had happened."

"Oh, boy," Jonathan shook his head. "We're a pair, aren't we? Me and her?"

"I guess, but want to hear something funny?" Joseph said to his brother.

"What"

"After Abby and I went back to Francine's house with her I walked down the street a little bit to say goodnight to Abby since she was staying the night there; to get some privacy, you know? Anyway, I was kissing her goodnight and she stopped and said to me, 'I hope we wind up just like them' – meaning you and Francine. I thought she meant fighting and not talking and all that so I asked why she would say something like that 'cause it didn't make sense, but she said to me: 'No, I mean so much in love that they'll be able to make it through *anything* and be together forever.' "

After digesting what Joseph said, Jonathan asked:

"She really said that?"

"Uh-huh."

Jonathan couldn't think of anything to say in reply.

* * *

Jonathan hesitated for a split second before dialing the final two digits – '37' – in Francine's phone number. Part of his hesitation was because he had only gotten several hours of mostly troubled shuteye after finally falling asleep around 3:30 in the morning, and with his brain a bit foggy he was struggling a bit to be certain about the Donners' phone number before he finished dialing. He didn't want to call a wrong number at 7:30 in the morning.

A ring and a half from the other side, and then a hesitant "Hello?"

Francine. Jonathan wondered if her night had been as restless and sleep-deprived as his.

If the matter hadn't been such a serious one, it might have been comical for someone listening to the conversation to hear Jonathan and Francine trample all over each other's words as they each rushed to apologize...repeatedly. Francine agreed that despite the early hour Jonathan could come over to her house.

"My mother talked to my father last night," she said in barely audible tones. When Jonathan pressed her for exactly what that meant she would only say "I'll tell you later" before they hung up.

Irene Coleman was already up and bustling about her kitchen. This was, after all, Thanksgiving Day and *this* was where Irene was most in her element. She had already dragged a sleepy Charlene from her bed and mother and daughter were busy at work on hotcakes for breakfast; dressing the turkey; and a host of other activities for the day's feasts.

Jonathan walked into the kitchen and over to his mother, who peered back at him with a look on her face that said "I may not like what you're about to do, but I suppose I understand." He kissed his mother on her cheek and then, in an unusual gesture, did the same to his sister. After he exited the kitchen Charlene looked at her mother and saw that tears were starting to gather in her eyes. Charlene put down the mixing bowl that was in her hands and walked over to her mother to give her a hug.

Irene looked at her daughter with surprise and Charlene said in response,

"I know this Thanksgiving isn't turning out exactly like you planned with Jonathan and Francine, and me and the War Bond show; even Joseph and his new girl. But please be happy for us, okay?"

Irene, afraid she would start crying if she tried to speak, could only muster a nod in return.

* * *

Jonathan had just reached the bottom step of the Donner house when the front door opened and out came a bundled-up Francine, who quickly bounded down the stairs.

"Let's go for a short walk," she said as soon as she reached the bottom.

"It's pretty cold out," Jonathan said. The temperature was slightly under forty but with the morning's faint light still trying to push through the sooty clouds, it felt at least ten degrees colder.

"It's okay," Francine said and hooked her left arm under Jonathan's right as she steered both of them down the street. They walked in silence for several minutes, occasionally glancing over at each other but neither uttering a word. Finally, Francine broke the silence.

"Last night before I went to find Abby and Joseph my mother asked why I was crying so hard, and I told her about our fight and that you had gotten all mad because my mother made me promise not to tell my father what happened with Donnie."

Jonathan was about to interrupt and object to Francine's statement that he was angry because of what Mrs. Donner had done – the last thing he wanted was her mother also to dislike him – but Francine continued her tale.

"After I got back from finding Abby and Joseph, my mother took me aside after Abby came in with me and said that she had told my father some of what happened last year."

"What do you mean 'some of what happened?' " Jonathan's eyes narrowed.

Francine shrugged.

"I asked her the same thing and all she would say was that she couldn't bring herself to tell my father everything she knew, but she did tell him enough so he would know that you hadn't done anything wrong."

Jonathan tried to process what Francine was telling him but Francine kept talking.

"My father was still awake and he sent Abby into the kitchen with my mother and sat me down in the living room. He said something like 'Your mother said that boy didn't do anything bad to you last year, so maybe I was too hard on him.' Something like that, I don't remember the exact words since I was still very upset, you know?"

Jonathan could only think: Jack Donner referred to him as "that boy?" Almost as if he wasn't worthy of bearing a name?

Francine stopped, unhooked her arm from Jonathan's, and turned to look at him.

"I honestly don't think my father will ever *really* like you because he would have to admit he was wrong, and I've never heard my father do that. I can't even believe that he would say that maybe he was too hard on you; that's about as close to an apology as I think I'll ever hear from my father. But after my mother talked to him, he doesn't think any more that you're this horrible man who did something terrible to his little girl."

She looked away for a moment and then back at Jonathan.

"I hope that's enough, and to be honest it's probably better than your mother will ever think of me because she knows what I did and will never forgive me; right?"

Jonathan thought for a moment.

"I don't know," he replied. "I think she's starting to realize what my Pop and I were talking about the other morning, that so many things are different because of the war, and maybe it's best to look past things now that you might have stayed mad about before the war. So yeah, she probably would have rather had me not see you at all while I was home and *definitely* not go out with you and...you know, but I think she will accept it because it's what I wanted to happen and it makes me happy."

Francine smiled.

"Does it make you happy? I mean, do I make you happy? Despite our fight on the phone last night?"

Jonathan was nodding even before she finished her rapid-fire questions.

"On the train ride all the way home, I kept thinking about you. I never thought we would actually go out on a date and talk about putting what happened behind us, but I kept hoping that we would run into each other and at the very least I could apologize for what I said to you back in February, and that maybe we would go for a cup of coffee and talk about the good times we had. And then I kept thinking about all those good times and I was so down in the dumps because they were over, but I still wanted to see you. I kept looking for you at Saint Michael's on Sunday when we..."

"Me too!" Francine interrupted. "I saw you and Joseph when I looked back as I was going home and wanted to find some excuse to go back, but then I figured I would see you soon enough and this way your mother and everyone else wouldn't be around."

Jonathan and Francine began walking again to fight off the chill and kept talking as they strolled along. A couple of minutes later Jonathan abruptly stopped.

"Last night after the movie, I mean if we had gone, I was going to take you up the incline to Mount Washington so we would have a special place where I asked you to marry me. But just like when I'll be on a mission before too long, if we can't get to the primary target we find a backup target."

He looked around, and then back at Francine as he reached into the left pocket of his A-2 flight jacket.

"So we'll always remember that I asked you to marry me in front of Cindy Zelenko's house, right?"

He flipped open the lid of the velvet box, removed the ring, and dropped to his right knee as he said the words to Francine Donner that he had originally planned to say eleven months earlier.

*   *   *

Jonathan wanted to wait on the Donners' front porch for several moments while Francine broke the news to her parents, but she insisted that he be right by her side when she told them that they were engaged.

Sally Donner seemed genuinely happy for her daughter; not simply because she realized this was what Francine wanted, but since all along she had known the full story about what had happened last year, and since Jonathan had apparently decided Sally's daughter was special enough to overlook what Francine had done with Jonathan's best friend, he must be a quality boy after all. The woman came across the living room to embrace her daughter and then also gave Jonathan a quick hug as well before turning to her husband and forcefully saying,

"Isn't that wonderful news, Jack?"

Jack Donner worked in the Pennsylvania & Lake Erie railroad yards as a laborer but he was an intelligent man and he had filled in the blanks on his wife's sparse explanation about "Jonathan Coleman not being at fault; it was Francine who did something she shouldn't have." He had a pretty good idea what that "something" was that his little girl had done, but as fate would have it the delay of nearly a year before Jack Donner found out the truth also resulted in a very muted response on his part. If he had learned last year that Francine had done "something" with Donnie Yablonski he likely would have brought down his full wrath on his daughter; maybe even banished her to live with her aunt and uncle in West Virginia.

Now, however, as with Gerald Coleman (though he didn't know this, at least not yet) and so many others, the nearly twelve months that America had been at war had also changed Jack Donner's perspective on matters such as this one. He was ashamed that his daughter had showed such poor judgment but when he thought about it, eleven months had passed and she had lived a normal life; she went to work every day at the War Production Board; and, he realized, she had made a mistake that other girls made but of course had survived. She wasn't "ruined" or "spoiled" – it had happened, now it was over, and everyone moved on.

He looked at this young man, standing there in his Air Corps jacket next to his little girl, and thought that if Jonathan Coleman could use the passage of time as a reason to look beyond what Francine had done, then he not only could do the same but perhaps give the young flyer a chance.

He nodded at Jonathan Coleman – not a warm nod, but one of unspoken understanding – and then got up to give his daughter a congratulations hug. When they finally broke their embrace, he reached out his right hand to the young man who might be his son-in-law one day – if he survived the war – and shook hands with Jonathan.

* * *

"Pass the Chantilly Potatoes a la Patton," the sailor two seats to the left of Marty Walker said with a chuckle. The sailors of the *Augusta* were having a merry old time with the special Thanksgiving menu being served as the ship continued to glide towards Bermuda. Every sailor had been given a commemorative menu pamphlet bearing a special holiday message from the ship's Commanding Officer and Admiral Hewitt, the Task Force 34 Commander, along with a listing of the complete menu and its dishes all named in honor of some aspect or another of their successful role in *Operation Torch.*

"Yeah, if you slide over the..." – Marty Walker paused as he briefly looked at his own copy of the menu to make sure he got the name right – "...Chicken and Turkey en Casserole a la Hewitt." Meanwhile the sailor directly opposite Marty on the other side of the table was still working on his Cream of Tomato Soup a la Casablanca, while the sailor to his left was bantering with two others and wondering when the Apple Pie a la Michelier would be making an appearance.

To some of these sailors, many of the names assigned to the dishes and courses might as well have been Roosevelt, MacArthur, Nimitz...just names, no more. To others, such as Marty Walker, his post had put him in contact not only with some of the Naval Officers such as Admiral Hewitt – apparently of chicken and turkey casserole fame, at least for today – but also Army officers such as General Patton, who had been aboard the *Augusta* with Admiral Hewitt before going ashore to lead his troops against Rommel. Marty bantered with the other sailors, much as everyone in that particular serving group was doing as they celebrated Thanksgiving, but his thoughts would periodically detour off to wondering about not only what mission might come next but what other Admirals and Generals, if any, he might find himself coming in contact with as a radioman.

Thinking about flag officers also made him think about yesterday's nightmare following the U-Boat alarm and the ship going to General Quarters, and another one he had after he dropped off to sleep – despite doing his best to stay awake – around 5:00 this morning. In that later dream, Marty was in the drink not with his family but a cluster of nameless Admirals. Nazi Messerschmitts were coming around for yet another strafing run, determined to blast as many of these Navy Admirals as they could while they bobbed helplessly in the ocean. And Marty was right in the middle of them…

"A-ten-hut!" a deep voice boomed above the loud racket in the sailors' mess and more than three hundred sailors all dropped their utensils as they snapped to attention.

"As you were, men," Admiral Hewitt himself said as he entered the eating area.

"As you were," he repeated and when the sailors had resumed sitting – but not eating, nobody dared pick up a fork while the Admiral was among them – he continued.

"Men, I'll be very brief because I know you all want to get back to your Chicken and Turkey Casserole a la Hewitt," he said, triggering a wave of laughter among the sailors.

"Notice how I get the main dish named after me and General Patton only gets potatoes," he added, causing another ripple of amusement in the hall.

"Anyway," he continued when the laughter subsided, "I want you all to not only enjoy this Thanksgiving meal but to take a moment while you're here to make sure you read the message inside your brochures here." Admiral Hewitt held up a copy of the same commemorative brochure that Marty and each sailor had been consulting for the assigned names for the courses. The Admiral flipped open his copy, took a brief look at the page with the message – his very own – and then continued.

"Five times while this ship was in North Africa...five times you engaged the enemy and not only were responsible for the *Augusta* rendering a good account of herself against heavy fire, but miraculously the ship came through unharmed and there were no injuries at all among her crew during the fighting. I know that some of you may come from different faiths but regardless of your personal beliefs, I hope each one of you stops to give thanks to the divine providence that was with us the entire time."

He paused for a moment, sipped from an untouched glass of water he picked up off the table, then continued.

"We will very soon make port in Bermuda and then we will continue on to Norfolk. I will be leaving the *Augusta* in Norfolk and you will continue on to New York for refitting, and then...well, the fates will take you somewhere else next and hopefully the same divine providence that was with you in North Africa will follow you whenever you go."

The Admiral took another sip of water.

"I want to take this occasion while you are all gathered together, and I'll do the same for the Officers and then the other groups of men that will be gathered together later, to extend my thanks to you and to wish each and every one of you the best. What you did back there in North Africa will go down in history as the beginning of the end for the Nazis. Eisenhower, Patton, and Montgomery will defeat Rommel and North Africa will be ours. Hitler will realize that he's not invincible, and that what he was able to accomplish against overmatched countries such as Poland will simply not be possible against the United States. We've taken the fight to them and we will continue to do so over and over again until this war has been won!"

A rousing cheer went up among the sailors at Admiral Hewitt's words, and he waited until the ruckus subsided before continuing.

"We will all face danger again but as I mentioned, I firmly believe that we have divine providence on our side as we sail and march on to face and then vanquish the Nazis. And for those of you who may wind up fighting against Japan the same holds true. Look at what your comrades did at Coral Sea and Midway. The tide of this war has changed and even though we have many battles ahead of us we *will* prevail."

Another round of cheers from the sailors burst forth, and the Admiral waited until it was mostly quiet before concluding.

"This day of Thanksgiving is a special one each year in general for us in America, but this particular Thanksgiving of 1942 is an extra-special one; and even more so for those of you here on the *Augusta* and your comrades throughout Task Force 34 and also on the other ships that are back in North Africa with the Army boys. I know you all would rather be with your loved ones back home on this day but I hope every man here long remembers this day – where you were, and what you have accomplished – and that the pride you feel today is something you'll tell everyone about at your first Thanksgiving back home, whenever that will be, and that you'll never forget this moment."

Before the sailors could burst out in another round of cheering, the Admiral's adjutant bellowed out another "A-ten-hut!" command as Admiral Hewitt turned to depart the room. The men sprung to attention once again, but once the Admiral was gone, they plunked down and resumed partaking of their Thanksgiving bounty...including the platters of Baked Spiced Spam a la Capitaine de Vaisseau that were just now arriving in the dining area.

Marty Walker was still homesick, and the Admiral's words about everybody wishing they were with their loved ones only magnified that feeling. He was still very uneasy about those unsettling dreams of the aftermath of being torpedoed, and couldn't shake the feeling that maybe those nightmares were premonitions.

But for the moment at least; for the rest of this day, he was certain; and hopefully for a while longer, Marty Walker took Admiral Hewitt's words to heart and gave thanks to the divine providence mentioned in their brochure and spoken about by the Admiral for not only having done his small part to help bring about the beginning of the end of the Nazi tyranny they were all fighting, but for having come through this first taste of war unharmed.

*   *   *

The Thanksgiving feast at the Coleman house – where Marty Walker fervently wished he were instead of aboard the *Augusta*, the celebratory atmosphere following Admiral Hewitt's speech notwithstanding – was somewhat more reserved than that which the absent Marty was experiencing. Still, the mood throughout the *Augusta* of having survived the battle and triumphed over adversity was similar in many ways to that of the Coleman table in the aftermath of the controversies and unexpected occurrences of the past several days. The "battles" were all behind now, and it was time for each of them to give thanks.

Francine Donner was welcomed to the Coleman table for the next few hours, as was Abby Sobol. Both girls would celebrate Thanksgiving with the Colemans but then go back to their own families for their own celebrations, and then both return back to the Colemans' home sometime around 7:00 that evening. Both girls wanted to spend this final evening that Jonathan and Joseph would be at home with their sweethearts, and after their own family obligations were concluded they would be welcomed at the Coleman household for as long as they could all bear to stay awake. The train that would carry Jonathan and Joseph away from home and begin the boys' journey back to Arizona would depart Pittsburgh's Penn Station at 6:00 Eastern War Time sharp the following morning, and everyone realized that sleep would be in short supply for one and all this evening…but not a single one of them cared, of course.

Two extra places were added to the table for the girls and along with Stan and Lois Walker, Lorraine, and Calvin they all squeezed together with Gerald, Irene, and – for the final time until only the Lord knew when – all five of the Coleman children. They all were barely seated when Gerald Coleman cleared his throat and rose from his seat at the head of the table. Gerald was rarely one for speeches or even pronouncing a blessing over a meal himself; such benedictions were usually assigned to one of the older boys. But on this occasion, Gerald felt compelled to offer his thoughts to those gathered at his table.

"We've all been looking forward to this Thanksgiving for months now," Gerald began. "We hoped that Jonathan and Joseph would receive furloughs from their Air Corps training and be able to come home, and when their Ma received Jonathan's letter back in September to let us know they would be home, we were all very glad."

He cleared his throat again and continued.

"We all have a great deal to be thankful for this year. Last Thanksgiving the war hadn't started yet for us, and we were giving thanks that so far by then we weren't at war. But not long after that came Pearl Harbor and for a while almost all the news from the war was very bad. Then we started getting a little bit of good news here and there, and for the past month most of what we are hearing gives us hope that the worst is past. For that we all give thanks."

Gerald paused for a brief moment, unsure for a second or two if he wanted to continue with what he was about to say next. He decided to proceed.

"I had planned to give thanks for Jonathan and Joseph staying safe in the Air Corps training, and for having all five of our children gathered around this table today. But I also want to give thanks for what has happened in the past couple of days. Everyone here knows that Jonathan and Francine got engaged, and Joseph met Abby. Also that our Charlene will be on a War Bond tour with Dorothy Lamour and doing her part to help all the boys in uniform."

Gerald paused again. His words were coming out stilted; mechanical; void of emotion. Earlier this morning he had given a great deal of thought to what he would say this afternoon and as he mentally rehearsed his words, he tried to come up with phrasing that hopefully would not make his wife sad or angry. But in doing so, he realized only now as he was speaking, very little of what he truly felt was being conveyed to those gathered here.

The hell with it, Gerald thought to himself. He threw away his mental script and began speaking from the heart.

"Jonathan and Joseph will be leaving to go back to Arizona tomorrow," he began again, "and nobody knows when our entire family will be able to gather again for Thanksgiving or Christmas or Easter. We all hope and pray that the day will come soon, but we all know there is a war to be fought and it will be a while before it's all over. Until that day comes, this Thanksgiving – today – is our final time for all of us to gather together and be thankful for what we've received and to ask the Lord for what we would like to receive and be thankful for in the future. When the boys came home Sunday morning, none of us knew that today we'd all be sitting here with not only our family but also Jonathan's fiancé and Joseph's girl. None of us knew that our Charlene would have caught the eye of movie and theater people and be invited to go on a War Bond tour right after Christmas."

Gerald shot a quick look in the direction of his wife to see if she seemed about to explode, but Irene Coleman was still sitting there calmly, almost impassively.

"We should all give thanks that these things that none of us expected to happen did happen. Our boys will be going back to Arizona with these girls back home waiting for them, and that's something to be thankful for. Charlene will have the chance to visit New York and Washington and Philadelphia and perform to raise money for the war, and that's something else we should all be thankful for. As far as we know Marty is safe over in the war, and that's something to be thankful for."

He looked at Thomas and Ruthie, and then their cousins as well.

"I don't mean to leave out Thomas and Ruthie and Lorraine and Calvin. We're all thankful that Thomas and Calvin are too young right now for the war, and we pray that by the time they're older the war will be over and they won't have to follow their brothers. We're also thankful that Ruthie now doesn't only have an older sister to help her out once in a while, she has Francine and Abby also. And we're thankful that Lorraine can see her cousin Charlene helping out selling War Bonds and in a year or two also help out with the war, even if it's not with singing and dancing but with something else."

Gerald stopped to take a sip of water before his final sentence.

"Every one of us should be thankful as we sit around the table for this day, and we should all remember that this first Thanksgiving during the war was a special one when we were blessed to have everyone except for Marty with us."

As he sat down Gerald felt badly about his "except for Marty" remark but he felt he had to include that sentiment; he could hardly give thanks that the "entire family" was gathered together without mentioning that Marty wasn't among them but instead was away at war, even though he was so very thankful himself that all five of his children were here this day.

With the conclusion of Gerald's speech, platters of food began to be passed around the table. Irene and Lois Walker frequently rose from the table to retrieve additional dishes from the kitchen, occasionally assisted by Charlene and Lorraine. The discussion mirrored that of Sunday's feast – war news mostly ignored during the celebration in lieu of happier topics – and attempts were made by almost everyone to include Francine and Abby in the conversation. There was plenty of discussion about the goings-on over at the War Production Board in general and at the field office in Oakland where the girls worked, with speculation about what the next rounds of regulations and reallocations might be in early 1943. Another scrap metal drive had been initiated the previous month and Abby was doing secretarial assistance for the man in charge of running the effort in Pittsburgh, and she related a few tidbits about how effective the drive had been so far in the city. Francine, for her part, was assigned to type and file memorandums related to steel production in the Pittsburgh area. She was privy to sensitive information about the industry's performance and was sworn to secrecy about specific facts and figures, but she was able to generalize to those gathered at the table that 1942's output thus far from Western Pennsylvania's mills was astonishing and had surpassed even the most optimistic projections.

Gerald, Stan, and the boys all leaned back with the same bloated bellies they had gladly suffered on Sunday. Shortly after 3:30, Irene and Lois began clearing the table and enlisted Charlene, Lorraine, and Ruthie in the effort. Francine hesitated a moment before asking if she and Abby could help, and after a moment's hesitation Irene nodded her consent...her way of signaling to Francine that the first small steps of including this girl into her family had just been okayed.

Francine and Abby helped for about a half hour and then departed for their own houses as planned. Jonathan and Joseph offered to escort their girls home but both Francine and Abby insisted the boys stay put as their remaining hours at home ticked away. The men and boys adjourned to the living room and flicked on the Philco to catch the end of the Duquesne football game against Lakehurst Naval Air Station, with the Dukes shutting out the Navy fliers from Jersey 13-0.

By 6:00 all of the kitchen work had been completed. At 6:30 – a half hour earlier than expected – Francine returned, and Abby arrived fifteen minutes later. As planned, the "early Christmas" for Jonathan and Joseph was convened and the boys each received their baseball mitts that their father had made by hand. Charlene had coordinated the gifts for her brothers that were also from Thomas and Charlene: two engraved silver Zippos bearing not only their names but also the inscription of "USAAF" on the second line and then, on the third line, "Thanksgiving, 1942."

Finally, their mother gave each of her sons a silver-framed color photograph of the entire Coleman family that had been taken the day of Joseph's high school graduation back in June. "You'll put these up in your barracks back in Arizona and then wherever they send you," Irene was able to choke out despite the lump in her throat as she handed the pictures to her boys.

They all spent the next several hours listening to the special Thanksgiving programming on NBC Red. Finally around 9:00 Lois and Stan departed with Calvin and Lorraine. They would not be coming to the train station in the early morning hours so each said goodbye to Jonathan and Joseph, with Lois Walker fighting back the tears as she did. Another hour passed and then Francine and Abby reluctantly rose to walk back to Francine's house. Jonathan and Joseph escorted their girls there, paused a few moments for sad goodnight kisses, and then returned home. They would both have liked to spend hours longer with their girls, but they knew that with their time at home running short every minute they could spend with their family was a treasured gift, and the girls would be accompanying them to the train station early in the morning to see them off.

The boys were both back inside the door of the Coleman house by 10:30, shaking off the late November chill before squeezing back onto the sofa with Thomas and Ruthie – who insisted on remaining awake a little while longer – between them. Charlene was sitting in one of the chairs by the radio, as was Gerald. Irene was still bustling back and forth between her kitchen and the living room, shuttling plates of pie and cups of piping hot coffee to her husband and her children.

None of them wanted this evening to end. Irene was walking back to her kitchen with Jonathan's and Joseph's empty pie plates when she heard the radio announcer say:

"Next up is Dorothy Lamour's recording of the song that Bob Hope and Shirley Ross performed in *The Big Broadcast of 1938*, a movie that Miss Lamour was also in. Here's *Thanks for the Memory*."

Irene froze just before she was about to push open the kitchen door. She turned around slowly and took in the scene in the living room: her husband and all five of her children, seated together listening to the radio. She felt the moisture come to her eyes as she watched and listened. None of her children noticed their mother staring at them and wishing that this vision never had to end, and also praying that one day she would see it again. But about halfway through the song Gerald Coleman happened to look up, see his wife looking back at them, and felt his own eyes become watery as he gazed around at all of his children and listened to *Thanks for the Memory*.

ABOUT THE AUTHOR

Alan Simon is the USA TODAY bestselling author of several historical novels set in the mid-20th century: **The First Christmas of the War, Thanksgiving, 1942, The First Christmas After the War,** and **Unfinished Business**. He is also the author of the USA TODAY bestseller **Gettysburg, 1913: The Complete Novel of the Great Reunion** about the 1913 "Great Reunion" that was held exactly 50 years after the Battle of Gettysburg and which was attended by more than 50,000 aging Civil War veterans.

Alan is also the author of the memoir **Clemente: Memories of a Once-Young Fan - Four Birthdays, Three World Series, Two Holiday Steelers Games, and One Bar Mitzvah,** published in honor and memory of the 40th anniversary of baseball Hall-of-Famer Roberto Clemente's tragic loss on a humanitarian mission.

He is a native of Pittsburgh (where several of his novels are set) and currently lives in Phoenix.

Enjoy the 3rd book in one family's wartime home front saga:

Christmas, 1945.

The terrible years of war are finally over and millions of American soldiers, sailors, and airmen will be reunited with their families just in time for this glorious holiday season.

Irene and Gerald have a special holiday gathering planned as the family gathers together to celebrate a family wedding along with:

The First Christmas After the War

and coming soon, the fourth title in our series:

A new decade...a new war. What will the outbreak of the Korean War mean to the Coleman family?

The First Winter of the New War

Would you like to be notified when **THE FIRST WINTER OF THE NEW WAR** is available? Email us at info@alansimonbooks.com to be included on our notification list, or visit http://www.alansimonbooks.com.

91955408R00125

Made in the USA
Lexington, KY
28 June 2018